Dorothea Benton FRANK

The
Christmas
Pearl

AVON

An Imprint of HarperCollinsPublishers

This book was originally published in hardcover November 2007 by William Morrow, an Imprint of HarperCollins Publishers.

Artwork appearing on pages 246-247 is from the Collections of the South Carolina Historical Society.

AVON BOOKS
An Imprint of HarperCollins*Publishers*
10 East 53rd Street
New York, New York 10022-5299

Copyright © 2007, 2009 by Dorothea Benton Frank
ISBN 978-0-06-143848-6
www.avonbooks.com

First Avon Books paperback printing: November 2009
First William Morrow hardcover printing: November 2007

Avon Trademark Reg. U.S. Pat. Off. and in Other Countries, Marca Registrada, Hecho en U.S.A.
HarperCollins® is a registered trademark of HarperCollins Publishers.

Printed in the U.S.A.

10 9 8 7 6 5 4 3 2 1

$\mathcal{A}$CKNOWLEDGMENTS

The energy and contagious enthusiasm of many people went into the creation of this book and I would like to thank them here. First and foremost, my gratitude to Buzzy Porter, who encouraged me to write this story in the first place, and to the South Carolina Historical Society for the use of the photographs of Charleston from ages ago. Huge thanks to Carrie Feron, my brilliant editor, who might be the most charming Yankee I have ever met except for Larry Kirshbaum, my fabulous agent, who is also a genius. Much love to both of you.

To the Morrow team with love and thanks: Jane Friedman, Michael Morrison, Lisa Gallagher, Virginia Stanley, Carla Parker, Carl Lennertz, Michael Morris, Michael Spradlin, Brian Grogan, Michael Brennan, Rhonda Rose, Donna Waitkus, Dale Schmidt, Liate Stehlik, Adrienne DiPietro, Richard Aquan, Tom Egner, Barbara Levine, Rick Harris, Ana Maria Allessi, Debbie Stier, Ben Bruton, Lynn Grady, Tavia Kowalchuk, and of course, always special thanks to Tessa Woodward.

To Debbie Zammit, Ann Del Mastro, and Kevin Sherry for endurance and friendship.

All my love to Peter, William, and Victoria. And to booksellers and readers everywhere—my holiday wish for you is one of perfect health and peace with my most heartfelt thanks for your support. Happy holidays and thank you, thank you, thank you!

The Christmas Pearl

Part One

· December Twenty-third ·

When I was a young girl, the glorious celebrations of the Christmas season were a very different affair than they are today. Of course, I am as old as Methuselah. Ninety-three. When I got out of bed this morning, every bone in my body creaked like the loose boards in the front staircase of this ancient house. Can you even imagine what it would be like to have lived so many years? It was hard to believe that I had done it myself. But there it was. I was an old nanny goat at last. However, I *much* preferred to be thought of as a stylish dowager, the doyenne of Murray Boulevard, staving off her dotage. The fact was that if *dotage* and incapacitating decrepitude couldn't take me down in ninety-three years, I might squeak my way to Glory unscathed. Hallelujah! Another blessing!

My, my! The world has certainly changed, although many other, more important things have remained the same. After all, as *Charlestonians*, we are the self-appointed guardians of all traditions worthy of preservation. For example, it was 2006, I was *still* living in my family's home, as my mother and grandmother had done. Probably my great-grandmother before them, too. My memory is a little bit fuzzy about that. Regardless, the point is, I never left. Why would I?

Unfortunately, our home has become a little threadbare. Everything from the plaster to the plumbing could use some attention. It was not that my offspring or their offspring couldn't gather the resources to correct the creaks and leaks; it was that no one seemed to be worried about how this state of dilapidation looked to outsiders. What kind of Charlestonian no longer cared about appearances? Apathetic slackers, I'm afraid to say. It made me sick in my heart. The house deserved better.

Like many classic Southern stately homes, ours has massive white Corinthian columns strung along the front portico. The foundation and the portico flooring is handmade brick, as is most of the entire house. My parents loved wrought-iron work so much that they added lots of detail—handrails, a balcony, and so forth.

Each generation—that is, until now—added some distinction to the house and grounds. I was the one who commissioned the gates forged by

Charleston's greatest blacksmith, Phillip Simmons, himself! Yes, it's true. I will never forget the day he came with his men to install them on the sidewall of the house. They are superb, like black iron lace, with delicate snowy egrets set in ovals in the center of each side. He brought with him a small plaque bearing his name—P. SIMMONS. He asked me if I thought it was all right to affix it to the bottom. I said, you go right ahead, Mr. Simmons, because you are truly an artist! So he did.

In the yard are sprawling magnolia and live oak trees dripping with great sheers of Spanish moss. In the rear gardens are azalea and camellia bushes that are as old as Noah's house cat. Most of the landscaping is original to the house, except for the few things we lost during hurricanes, disease, or because of hostile visitors, if you know what I mean. Naturally, we have fig ivy crawling up the front steps that grows so quickly it makes me wish I carried pruning shears in my purse. Truth? Everything needs pruning and a good coat of paint.

I shouldn't dwell on it. What was I supposed to do about renovations and repairs when my life had come to a place where I was practically a guest in my own home? Not much, I'm afraid. In any case, I was determined to maintain a positive attitude.

I was preparing to celebrate Christmas with my darling daughter, Barbara, her family, and their spouses and children, who had all arrived for the holidays. To give you the family map, Barbara and her husband, Cleland, who are both in their early sixties, live here with me. Their grown children have children and live in their own homes in Atlanta and Charlotte. I'm slightly embarrassed to admit that I'm glad they do. Bless their hearts, they are a truculent bunch. Yes, they are, but I mean that in the nicest possible way.

It might interest you to know how the house retaliated against their presence. Every time my whole family gathers under this roof, the walls rattle, the chandeliers downstairs flicker, and every portrait goes crooked on its nail. You see, along with the living comes the dead. Yes, our house is very haunted. It certainly is. Or it is sinking. Or perhaps both. I was never quite certain which because Charleston, especially the tip of the peninsula where we live, was built on plough mud. However, I can see Fort Sumter from my bedroom window. Knowing all that the mighty fortress represents gives me ample strength to deal with them.

All I can do all day is cluck to myself. I am clucking for a good reason. This was supposed to be a time of great joy. Unfortunately, Barbara's family always does such a pitiful job of the production of our Christmas celebration that I wind up disheartened. In her defense, at her age Barbara can only do so much on her own and the rest of them are clueless. Sadly, no one else appears to see anything wrong with the ramshackle way things are thrown together. Truly, I don't mean to judge them so harshly, but somehow it seems to me that they have allowed the whole spirit of the season to erode into blatant commercialism. I could have told them plenty of ways to revive the beauty of the past. I have tried many times; however, who wants to listen to an old coot like me? I worry that it is too late. When I close my eyes for the last time, an entire library of instructions for genuinely rewarding living will go with me.

It isn't that they do not *think* their efforts are sufficient. My opinion? They surely aren't creating anything for one another that comes even remotely close to the wonderful memories I have. Maybe I am looking at them with a jaundiced eye. For the life of me, I just can't *feel* their excitement. Their Christmas plans seem to have become little more than a burden and a bother. Everything is rush, rush, rush!

I know I've been a lucky woman. In the holiday seasons of my youth, back in the early twentieth century, my brother and I believed anything, *anything* at all, was possible. Christmas was charmed. There is simply no other or better way to say it.

Imagine *this*. My parents, my brother, and I all lived with my grandparents right here because my grandparents *wanted* us to. Do tell! We got along just fine. Usually, that is. On a rare occasion I caught my father's sleeve as he stormed out through the front door. I would ask him if he was angry. He would knit his eyebrows, say no, he would be back in a while, that he was going up to the Hibernian to talk his friend out of having another drink. Oh my! How funny to remember the clever way he phrased his discontent! He didn't have disagreements with anyone too often. None of us did. Harmony really *was* the norm. Why? I have to say that it was all a result of Pearl's tutelage and, heaven knows, her perseverance.

Pearl drilled it into our skulls that it was extremely important to love and cherish one another. She would say, there are enough people to argue with *out there*—meaning the outside world. She would flip upside down and spin sideways in her grave to see how my family behaves today.

It is true that like a lot of older people, I romanticize the past. With so little effort I can relive those days like they were only moments ago. In my mind's eye, I look back over my shoulder. There is my youth at the end of an extremely long foggy tunnel dug through time, hung with gossamer veils. All I have to do is swing those veils aside to clearly see and remember how things really were. And it was wonderful.

What was my best Christmas? That would be a difficult choice to make, but there *is* one in particular that stands out from the others. My mother was still alive. The year was 1920, I think. Yes, that's right: 1920. I would have been just six years old and in the first grade. There was a lot happening in the *real* world. The real world was that dull place where the adults seemed to orbit on another planet.

Although I was terribly small, I was still aware of the headlines of the day. We had a copy of Charleston's *News & Courier* in our house every day of the week. But to tell you the truth, I didn't care much about the news, as it had little or no effect on me. I knew that the war in Europe was finally ended because that terrible war had been the main topic of discussions around the dinner table since I could remember any conversations at all. At last there was peace. The adults said with long, whooshing sighs of relief that the economy was getting better, that the civilized world was finally putting itself back together again. They said this about a million times, as though there were nothing else to talk about.

In my local realm, all the boys in my school, my brother included, were baseball crazy. I didn't think it was so great that Babe Ruth was going to join the Yankees. Yankees? Were they serious? Or did I give one toot that Edith Wharton had just published *The Age of Innocence*? I was having my *own* age of innocence and hopping from foot to foot waiting for Christmas to arrive!

Christmas! May I just tell you what it was like? Oh my! The air positively crackled with excitement. Starting at our home, anticipation and optimism spewed from every corner of Charleston as though all the water pipes were springing pinhole leaks, one after another, all across the city. In succession, not secession. That was a little joke.

The holidays! Grown-ups met their friends at all manner of gatherings, people whom, perhaps, they hadn't seen all year. Small gifts were exchanged, cards were sent and received, and the doorbell rang all the time. People dropped by to see my grand-mother and mother, who did many charitable things for others, just to say they wished us well. Some brought us red poinsettias, which Mother would group around the sides of the fireplaces. Others came with a box of homemade fudge or taffy that would go in a crystal dish on the dining-room sideboard whose cover betrayed us with a tinkle every time we reached in for a treat.

"You chillrun get your hands outta there, 'eah?" Pearl would call out from another room. "You'll ruin your supper!"

That woman could hear a handkerchief flutter to the ground from all the way across town. She surely could.

The parade of visitors seemed endless to my brother and me. We would race to the door hoping it was a candy delivery from a friend of our par-ents and not another useless poinsettia. Gordie and I were the recipients of endless head pats and cheek pinchings, and the well-wisher would invari-ably say that my grandmother Dora never seemed to age, that my mother, Helena, was just like her, but, my oh my, how Gordie and I had grown. We would smile politely at them, roll our eyes at each other, only to steal away as soon as possible to resume whatever parlor game we had been playing in between chores. Gordie was a fidgeter extraordinaire. What child wasn't when the holidays were within his reach?

The preparations for the season were such an enormous undertaking that everyone rolled up their sleeves, pitching in to help. It began weeks before Thanksgiving, lasting the whole way through the bone-chilling gray days of January, when Pearl, with that sly look of hers, would surprise us with the last slice of fruitcake she had squirreled away somewhere. She would share it with Gordie and me over cups of hot tea spiced with orange rinds and cloves.

Pearl was my grandmother's housekeeper/ manager/caterer/psychiatrist/best friend without whom our lives surely would have collapsed. Well, she wasn't actually a licensed psychiatrist. She was an excellent listener, dispensed sound advice for every situation, and she was right every single time. She was naturally brilliant, very mysterious, and whenever she was around, you could always smell a trace of blackberries in the air. She had eyes in the back of her head because Gordie and I never got away with a single bit of naughtiness unless she wanted us to. When she got excited, Pearl spoke

Gullah. When she was feeling blue, she told me true stories her mother had told her about slavery that frightened me and distressed me so that I cried for hours. She was my favorite person in the world, the one I wanted to please most. Especially after Mother died.

From our perspective, Pearl was as imposing as a statue of George Washington. She had to be more than six feet tall, portly, her salt-and-pepper-streaked hair slicked back into a bun at the nape of her neck. Every single day she wore a freshly starched, black cotton dress with a long white apron. When my grandmother or my mother entertained, she wore a different apron with a ruffled edge. She also bobby-pinned a small white starched linen tiara into her hair. Just her presence was enough to scare the day-lights out of most people, but we knew she loved us with the same fierce love we felt for her. And me? I lived in her shadow, never out of her earshot.

The fact that the house belonged to my grand-mother was of no significance to me because Pearl was the engine that made every good thing happen to us and for us. Especially as she commandeered *the mission* of creating the holiday season's grand affairs.

First, there was the arrival of nuts. A childhood

friend of my father's who lived way up in Sumter had a grove of paper-shell pecan trees. Every year a twenty-pound burlap sack of them would find its way to the shade of our back door. Sometimes we got other varieties, but moist, buttery paper-shell pecans were our favorite. They were a treasure, to be sure. Daddy always tried to give his friend some money for them, but he would firmly resist. Finally Daddy would say that they should smoke a cigar together and toast the holiday with a little glass of O Be Joyful. They would sit for a spell, just drinking and visiting, laughing, retelling stories of their shared childhood and how they learned to fish or hunt.

Clearly the advent of the pecans was the trigger for the festivities of the season.

Pearl would say, "It's time to crack some nuts. Y'all gwine help."

Of course I jumped right to it. It made me feel very grown up. She would help me tie on an apron. I would sit on a high stool in the kitchen, cracking them with a handheld metal nutcracker, letting them drop right into a large yellow bowl. Later Pearl and I would sift through them, discarding the shells, inspecting them with a steel pick, carefully removing the bitter woody shards that lined the grooves of the nut meats. The cleaned nuts would be stored in airtight glass canisters until we had enough to make all the holiday recipes, the same ones we made every year.

Whole pecan halves were separated from broken ones and later pressed into fondant, a sweet holiday candy like fudge that Pearl would dye pale pink or green. More nuts would be slipped inside of dates, rolled in powdered sugar, or cooked in butter, sprinkled with granulated and dark brown sugar. Tiny pieces were mixed into rum balls or sands. The rest were chopped up for nut cakes and fruitcake. Of course Gordie, being a normal boy who loved to cut up the fool, would snitch a rum ball, eat it, then pretend to be drunk, weaving around the kitchen bumping into things. I would be carried away with giggles until I fell to the floor with him. Even Pearl would smile and shake her head. Believe it or not, the fruitcakes of my youth were *delicious*. No one made jokes about substituting *them* for bricks or footballs.

There are none in 2006. Everyone is on a blooming diet or watching their cholesterol or some other fool thing.

Did we decorate? Mercy! This old house sprang to life, breathing pride and contentment with the trimming we did for the holidays. A week after Thanksgiving, Pearl, Gordie, and I would gather together on the back porch with Mother. First, we put long pieces of rope in the old tin washtub and soaked them in water overnight. The weather was usually mild enough to wear just a sweater. We wore old gardening gloves, as it was kind of a sloppy business. Working as a team, helping one another, we would construct thick majestic garlands, heavy with pine, cedar, and magnolia, discreetly tucking the small branches in between the twists of water-soaked rope. When the rope dried, they held tight. We were positive our garlands were fit for a palace.

When Pearl or our mother measured, remeasured, and determined that one had reached the proper length, one of them would clip the rope and knot the end. Together, we would carry them inside, carefully, in a great procession, like long Chinese paper dragons, placing each one in some part of every room in the house. The staircase banisters were swagged, mantels were draped, garlands were hung around every doorway; we looped long pieces around the great-hall mirror that reached from the floor to the ceiling, and of course another one framed the front door outside. Naturally, there were wreaths made of greens and small pieces from a bush we called popcorn, because the small berries were lumped together and white. Sometimes we tied in baby pinecones, sprigs of holly with red berries, or lady apples when we could find them. We always had wide red satin ribbon, the same ribbon we saved from year to year, which Pearl would unpack and unroll. She would sing gospel music, like "Come en Go wid Me," which was telling everybody to ask for Jesus to come again. When she forgot a word or two she would hum while she gently ironed out the wrinkles from where the bows had been tied in prior years.

We all had our jobs to do. I'll confess, some were more pleasant than others. Gordie and I didn't mind wiping the magnolia leaves with an old dishcloth spotted with corn oil to make them look like patent leather, but neither one of us enjoyed getting the sticky pinesap all over our faces and arms. Somehow we always got blotches of it on us. My mother would scrub us in our old claw-foot bathtub until we howled for freedom. Gosh! I haven't thought about that in years! Gordie surely could howl like a wild man.

No one makes garlands today. Or wreaths. Everything is ordered from the florist or a catalog or bought on the side of the road from the same fellow who sells fireworks in the summer. Or even more terrible, people use plastic fake things that give your home no fragrance at all. I find this very disappointing. You have to understand that the real fun of the season was in the *preparation*. The preparation fueled our frenzy of anticipation.

Naturally there were gifts. Gordie and I would construct bookmarks for our mother and grand-mother. They loved to read. Our home was well stocked with books of every kind. We'd draw a flower or a bird on a long skinny piece of stiff paper, color it carefully, then fringe the bottoms with manicuring scissors. The other side was then signed and dated. The bookmarks were enclosed in handmade cards. We hid everything under our beds until the tree went up.

A crisp morning would find us walking up King Street to Kerrison's Department Store hand in hand with Pearl. With what little money we had earned by performing small chores like sweeping the steps or folding towels, we would argue and finally settle on a linen handkerchief or a necktie for our father. Later a card would be made for him, too. What to give Pearl was always a huge dilemma. Gordie or I would pester someone into shopping with us to find her a nice pair of gloves, a sweater, or a pretty scarf that would be from us. It seems to me now that way back then, the other adults made us *work* for their attention and affection. Pearl freely gave an abundance of both. Maybe there was a lesson there—a pearl of wisdom?

Anyway, the whole business took *weeks* to accomplish! When it was over, the house was festooned to a fare-thee-well and we were ready to be fattened up with all the goodies we had made to eat. By the time the Christmas tree was up and decorated, Gordie and I were bug-eyed trying to catch a glimpse of anything that might resemble a reindeer and our ears were peeled for the jingle of any kind of bell.

We had a beautiful crèche set that was carefully arranged on the ancient mahogany entrance-hall table with votive candles nestled in more greens. In retrospect, it was probably a fire hazard! No one seemed to worry about those things then. You might ask why a Protestant household had a painted plaster crèche set. It had been given to us by a Catholic friend of my grandmother. She said it was a beautiful reminder of what the entire holiday was about. She was right! There was just Joseph, Mary, an ox, and a donkey in a humble stable.

On Christmas morning we added the Baby Jesus, the shepherds that night, and then we took them away at the beginning of January when the kings arrived. The shepherds had to go back to work, didn't they?

The family Bible was opened on another table to a beautiful artist's rendering of the Nativity scene. Greens surrounded it just so in an Advent wreath of four candles, three purple and one rose-colored. They stood solemnly in shining brass candlesticks around the Bible, lit only at supper. One the first week, two the second . . . all leading up to the big event.

We were regular churchgoers, staunch believers in the true meaning of Christmas. Gordie? At his age? Be assured that he was in church and his eyes were squeezed tight while he petitioned the Lord for cowboy guns or a catcher's mitt. I was right next to him, hands folded thumb over thumb, fingers pointed toward heaven, fervently pleading for a doll that said "mama." Since we finally had peace on earth and there seemed to be a lot of goodwill toward men, surely it was okay to ask God to help you out with Santa?

That's just how the holidays were. We cracked nuts, we made our own decorations and most of our gifts, we went to church, and we waited for Santa. Everyone baked for the holidays—sweets usually. Most people didn't decorate nearly as much as we did. I'm not sure if we tackled the season with such gusto because my grandmother, mother, and Pearl thought it would keep us busy and out of trouble or perhaps because *they* just couldn't stop themselves. It didn't matter. The house smelled delicious and looked gorgeous from all the greens and baking. Just the fact that we did these things together made us happier than I have ever been since.

Those days are long gone. Gordie, Pearl, my parents, and grandparents are all gone. My poor sweet husband, Fred, went to glory about ten years ago and I still miss him every day. Life surely is lonely without my darling Fred.

Gordie, who grew up to be a soldier and was every girl's sweetheart, died in Normandy, the French shores of the world's next terrible war. None of us ever recovered. How could we? We were proud and took some solace in the fact that our family had produced someone who died a heroic death, defending our Allies in Europe. Still, the loss of Gordie cut a hole in all of us. We bore invisible punctures of grief forever. My grandfather died when I was just barely out of diapers.

My grandmother went to heaven and then we lost Pearl. My beautiful mother died suddenly when I was thirteen. If my father were alive today, he would be one hundred zillion years old, so I'm not being morbid to speak of his demise. I mean, I miss them all. However, I'm not the kind of woman who gets maudlin, most especially over things I can't control.

It's just that things were vastly different then. I'll tell you this much. Pearl, even my mother, would be appalled by the fake trees and wreaths, inflatable Santas, and that the pecans are so astronomically priced, sold half cleaned and in ugly cellophane bags. Pearl would be deeply disappointed that no one seems to make, eat, or exchange cakes or candies or that handmade gifts are almost unheard of in today's world. Knit someone a sweater or crochet an afghan? Not anymore! They would be *especially* horrified that people give gift certificates via the Internet—whatever that is—that they think the fact that they spend a few dollars with a couple of clicks is an actual exertion. A great personal sacrifice! Priorities are hugely different in today's world. I imagine all this technology is useful in many endeavors. But like private education and small business, as you might have guessed I would have greatly preferred a handmade bookmark to a free meal at some chain establishment posing as a restaurant.

This is just me. Even though I feel as spry as I did, oh, thirty years ago, the fact is that I *am* an elderly lady. It is Christmastime again, everyone is here, and as I have pointed out, our crazy old house is giving us a dose of continuous holiday live theater, a protest from beyond the grave.

The walls are moaning, the pictures are askew, the lights are switching from dim to bright for no good reason at all except that the house itself or the ghosts in it doesn't like the way my daughter, her husband, my grandchildren and great-grandchildren are running their cockeyed show. I am just trying to stay out of their way.

Lying in bed at night, I privately admitted that a lot of the blame was mine. I was plenty vexed with myself for not encouraging Barbara the way Pearl pushed us to create holiday thrills. Here was something else I had been thinking about lately: I missed Pearl more than I missed my mother.

My mother loved the holidays, but she had Pearl to do everything while she saw to her social commitments. Yes, she would begin the season with us and liked to decorate, but as the parties rolled around, we seldom saw her. Sometimes I thought I hardly knew my mother at all. Losing her at thirteen was so traumatic that I struggled for years to remember the details of her face in my mind, and so photographs of her were that much more precious to me. I took an oath that I would always be available to my children.

Later on, when I married and took over the house, I never had someone like Pearl to work for me. I only had Barbara. I made my share of cupcakes, but I wasn't involved in activities outside the home. Barbara and Fred were easy enough to care for, and my father, who lived with us until his call to heaven, helped, too. Barbara was a quiet, understanding child who always seemed to find ways to amuse herself.

Now, don't go telling this, but there was a time when Fred and I worried that Barbara would never marry. It was around that time that the house started to moan. The house and its spirits wanted a guarantee that another family would take my place and Fred's when Saint Peter knocked on our door.

Poor Barbara! She had unfortunately inherited my grandmother Dora's pronounced nose and some other quirks and personality traits that would never make her the belle of the ball. Thank all the stars in the sky that there truly is a lid for every pot because when Barbara was about twenty, Cleland Taylor appeared on the scene with his boyish but patrician looks. Cleland was from a nice family, but was an unspectacular scholar who demonstrated a startling lack of ambition. However, he held a degree in political science from the University of Virginia and a job in a bank here in Charleston, rising to the position of manager—which in those days meant something more than it does today.

Privately, I would worry with Fred that Cleland's proposal of marriage to Barbara was based on financial security. Not love. He said I was a skeptic. My Fred, ever the diplomat, never missed an opportunity to point out any evidence of affection on Cleland's part. They finally made it down the aisle with our blessings. After a short honeymoon in San Francisco, they moved in with us, in the time-honored tradition of my family's history.

On the surface, Barbara's early years of marriage looked like mine—simple, quiet, orderly. The need for her to engage full-time help was never there, as I cooked and Fred was handy. More importantly, satisfactory talent never appeared on our doorstep. Women like Pearl didn't exist anymore.

When Barbara and Cleland's children came

along, George then Camille, sibling rivalry soon reared its ugly head. Barbara couldn't control their arguing, Cleland began to withdraw, and discontent became the order of the day. It was some sour pickle! The house had its next generation of tenants, but it was not satisfied with the temperature of their waters. So, no surprise to me, the house moaned and rattled, using Thanksgiving until well after New Year's Day to state its grievances.

By the grace of heaven and herculean struggles, Barbara brought George and Camille to adulthood then marriage. Each marriage has thus far born one grandchild. None of them are much to brag about so far because they have all sucked the life from my daughter. In my family, I love in order of birth and Barbara was there before all of them.

Even now, Barbara is plain-looking, not terribly fashionable, and painfully shy, but she has a heart of gold. Has that been enough to keep a petulant husband in line and to guide two difficult children? No.

It was my fault. I was the mother bird who never taught her hatchling to spread her little gray wings and fly. I had captained a rudderless ship, bound for the Land of Ennui. It was true. It was my mother's death and Pearl's shortly afterward that sabotaged my skills to imbue Barbara with what she needed. I knew what a mother was supposed to do up until a daughter was thirteen or so, but after that I was lost.

Enough of that! You can't get from ninety-three to ninety-four sloshing around in self-recriminations, can you? And Cleland is not without merit. He certainly held enough chairs and doors for me to satisfy anyone's definition of a gentleman. It's just that Fred and I had such high hopes for Barbara and Cleland and their children. I knew there was a basic goodness in them all; it was just that it seemed, well . . . what could I do to bring it out?

To preserve my sanity and bolster my spirits on a daily basis, I had developed my own routine to keep me not just young at heart, but also *young at mind*. I made it a point to inquire about Barbara's well-being and how things were at the bank for Cleland that day. I read the newspaper every morning so that I had something to discuss at the table that evening. Each night after supper, at precisely seven o'clock, I indulged myself with a moderate measure of bourbon over shaved ice mixed with a little sugar syrup, garnished with a sprig of fresh mint. Yes, a mint julep in my favorite cut-glass tumbler, which is so well used it seems to me the edges are finally wearing away. You could set your wristwatch by its arrival.

Eliza, who was our modern-day version of a part-time partner in crime, as Pearl had been to my grandmother and mother, brought it to me with a small linen napkin and two cheese straws on a tiny silver tray, the one Eliza and I liked best. It had been passed down to me by my great-grandmother. While it wasn't elaborate, it reminded me of more gentle days. Eliza liked the ceremony as much as I did. For me, it marked another victorious day aboveground. For her, it was the beginning of her evening at home away from us.

No one could make mint juleps like Eliza, who had prepared one delicious meal after another for our whole family for the past twelve years. After eighty-something years in the kitchen, I hired Eliza as a treat for all of us. I could take it easy. My sweet Barbara had never been terribly imaginative or successful in the kitchen, even with shelves of cookbooks at her disposal. Like the younger generations say? *Not happening.* Barbara was a dear and we had Eliza to keep us nourished. It wasn't that we couldn't cook; it was just that Eliza was a trained chef. When Eliza was there, the house was a happy place. Besides, let's face it. My social life was thin.

My generation had been diminished to almost zero by the general calamities of living. I am probably one of the oldest people in Charleston! Can you imagine how very peculiar that is? Some days I can feel death all around me, so I feel some urgency to enjoy myself as much as I can within the boundaries of propriety of course.

Holiday decorations were not in Eliza's job description. We accepted that. She did the grocery shopping, prepared dinner and supper, and cleaned up the kitchen. On occasion, Barbara used a cleaning service for the laundry and other general housework. But Eliza really gave the house the atmosphere we wanted.

Sometimes it seemed that I shared more secrets with Eliza than I did with my own daughter. She knew I valued her friendship and discretion enormously. Sometimes I would sit in the kitchen with her, but I wasn't working. Frankly, the last thing I needed was to fall on a wet floor. What if I broke my hip? So for that reason as well, I was very glad to have Eliza in my employ. Every day she came to work she might have been extending my life.

Between us? For some peculiar reason she was the only one of our entire congregation who recognized and agreed with me about the general dissatisfaction and antics of the house. Maybe that extrasensory sensitivity was a side benefit of being an authentic Lowcountry resident. Who could say?

So these were my thoughts and it was Christmas Eve again. I was alone in the dining room, dressed in my favorite green knit dress and jacket that I wore during the holidays. On my left shoulder was the little emerald-and-pearl circle pin that had been Fred's last gift to me. I touched it, remembering how he had smiled when he saw how thrilled I was by it, and how he pinned it to my shoulder. I waited for Eliza to arrive with my treat. I had to admit, I liked order and ritual more than ever. Habits surely contributed to keeping my beans together. The mint julep did not impair my tolerance level. In fact, it helped.

To be brutally honest, on this night of this particular year, everything was worse than ever. My heart was so troubled.

My family bickered across the hall in the living room as they decorated their so-called Christmas tree. I hesitated to join them. I simply didn't want to be a party to their shenanigans. At least not without some fortification, as they were almost intolerable. I had dreamed about their attitude, had I not? Yes, I had. So many nights, I would see Pearl's face in my dreams just shaking her head and wagging a finger at me.

There was my conundrum. I knew that the odds were that the Good Lord was going to call me home soon—no one lived forever. Except, I did not want to leave the earth with my family in its present state. What could I do? Who cared what an old lady thought?

"Here we are, Ms. Theodora! Just the way you like it!"

"Oh my! Thank you, Eliza!" I took the drink and the napkin and put the dish of cheese straws on the table. I motioned to the living room, where my family's voices cackled like crows above the beautiful music of Tchaikovsky's *Nutcracker*. "Listen to them, will you?"

We stood together, watching the lights flicker. Picture frames tipped to the east and west as we listened to them.

"They all need a good switching!" I said.

"They have always been like this," Eliza said. "At least, since I've known them."

"I think they're worse."

Well, there were a few blessings to count. Barbara and Cleland's son, George the Complainer, was finally delighted about something. Nine months and two days after they married, his third bride, Lynette, who is from an unfortunate family of greatly lesser means and manners, had given him a daughter.

Their child, Teddie, had been strategically named for me in hopes that when I went to my great reward, theirs would be greater. She was barely ten years old, a little devil, and had been right from the cradle. George spoiled her absolutely rotten and rarely corrected her.

I'm sorry to say, Lynette was too intimidated by George to be an effective disciplinarian. In addition, she was so thin she could blow away in a strong wind. I think that Lynette's weight was a direct result of George's vigilance about every crumb that traveled to her mouth. The world would say he was a very shallow man and excessively concerned with her appearance. Ah, well. Poor Lynette. George just had to have something to control and poor Lynette was it. Lynette wore what George liked, vacationed where George wanted to go, and George had the pitiful wisp dripping in diamonds. Their Teddie would probably have been an adorable child if she weren't the weapon they hurled at each other when the winds between them blew foul. George was a wildly successful real-estate broker. On top of everything else, I was certain that his success caused some jealousy between him and his father.

Camille, at thirty-six, was separated from her husband, Grayson, and was patently jealous of Lynette's jewelry and grander possessions. Their little boy, Andrew, who was a darling child, had suffered horribly from the separation. I would venture a bet that Andrew had a tutor for something or other every afternoon! Every time Grayson tried to exercise his right of visitation, Camille lit angry fireworks. It was very upsetting to everyone. She called Grayson such terrible names and said such vile things about him that I believed Andrew thought if he showed affection for his father, he was betraying his mother. And Camille really did baby him too much. It was just all so convoluted and wrong.

"They have everything in the world you could want," I said. "It makes me want to cry."

"I don't know, Ms. Theodora," Eliza said. "For some people, everything isn't enough. You want me to get some coal to put in their stockings?"

I knew that Eliza's little drop of levity was intended to keep my spirits afloat.

"If only coal would do the trick . . ." I sighed and looked at her. "Malcontents. That's what they are.

An ensemble of malcontents." I heard the portrait of my grandmother over the dining-room mantelpiece scrape the wall as it slid a little, and I stepped over to right it, giving her image a wink. I could almost hear her saying, *My poor dumbbells!*

Just then, Eliza's cell phone rang and she stepped away to answer it. I took another deep breath, a long swig, and went into the living room to see what I could do about the appalling way they were dressing the tree.

Where did all these new things come from? The tree's lights were blinking so fast and crazy I could not imagine how they could see where to place any of the ornaments without going cross-eyed. On closer inspection, I could see that the older ornaments, the ones we had collected since before I was born, had been relegated to the back of the tree. The front was covered in some crazy-looking elves with long legs like spaghetti, fat rhinoceroses dressed up like ballerinas, and every other kind of silly thing the world could dream up to shake money from your wallet.

They must have seen the shock on my face.

Camille said, "What the matter, Gran?"

"She doesn't like your wacky tacky glitter theme," Cleland said bluntly without apology.

Silently I agreed with him. I thought the new decorations were absolutely in the worst taste imaginable, but I also realized that I was a very conservative, traditional woman. Anyway, how could I be thrilled with a tree whose decorations, which represented more than a century of living, were shoved aside like an ugly blight?

True, it was still my house, but long ago I had allowed Barbara and Cleland to take over the day-to-day operations. I'm sorry and don't mean to whine, but I waited all year to touch each one of those ornaments and to remember where they had come from or who had given them to us. Maybe it was overly sentimental of me. I was feeling very melancholy. And if I said anything about it, one single word, I would just be adding pepper to the pot.

My poor spineless daughter, Barbara, meekly said, "Well, the White House has trees in every room and each one represents a theme. So I imagine if you want a new theme, Camille, why would anyone object? After all, we *did* decide over Thanksgiving that Camille would be in charge of the tree this year."

Quietly, I took a seat on the end of the sofa and decided again to hold my tongue. I did have the thought that I would not have put Camille in charge of making slice-and-bake cookies, which were another abomination of the immediate-gratification society in which we lived. She would forget the oven was on, leave the house, and it would burn down to the ground. After she burned the cookies, that is.

"Andrew is *such* a baby," Teddie said to me in her shrill voice from across the room. "He *still* believes in Santa Claus."

She repeated this several times until I worried that Andrew would start to wail. He was only eight and his beastly cousin was trying to ruin his Christmas. Just as I was on the verge of giving that child a piece of my mind, Camille spoke up.

Abruptly, she covered Andrew's ears and said, "Lynette? Can you please ask your daughter to stop?"

"Camille?" George said. "Why don't *you* shut up? Go take something to calm yourself down."

"Now see here," Cleland said in a stern manner, and then his patriarchal stance evaporated like morning dew as he said nothing more, went to the bar, and poured yet another drink.

In my opinion, Cleland drank too much. Once he had been quite the charmer, but over the years, he had withdrawn into himself and away from the family.

Well, that was enough, so I stood up with the intention of turning down the music. This time I was ready to give them the lecture they had earned. But before I could reach the remote control for the stereo, I turned to see Eliza in the doorway of the room, dressed in her coat and hat over her apron. She was quite upset.

"Whatever is the matter?" I said.

"My daughter's in labor . . ."

"But I thought the baby was coming in February," Barbara said, as though a baby had never been born prematurely in the history of humanity.

Oh Lord, no! I thought and sent up a silent prayer that she would be all right.

"The baby's breech. That was my son-in-law on the phone. He says she's calling loud for me!"

"Then you have to go!" Barbara said, redeeming every false start of her life, in my eyes at least. "Go and don't worry!"

"Barbara!" Cleland said in a shout. "You can't boil water! What about our dinner tomorrow and on Christmas?"

That was an example of the long reach of my son-in-law's sensitivity.

"I called my friend Jewel," Eliza said. "She says she'll come and help you tomorrow and on Christmas day!" Then Eliza burst into tears. "Ms. Theodora? Can I see you outside for a moment?"

"Absolutely!" I said, and hurried to her side.

I followed her as she moved quickly down the hall and through the kitchen to the back door. Her car was parked in the gravel courtyard behind the house.

She said, "She—Jewel, that is—she's kinda not so easy to get along with and she wants a terrible amount of money to do this job, it being Christmas and all. I'll pay you back, but I've *got* to go be with my girl! Please . . ."

"Don't you even think a thing about it," I said. "Any problem you can fix with a handful of money isn't a problem at all. Go! Scoot! Good luck and call me!" I was about to close the door when I remembered something and called, "Eliza!" I hurried down the steps to her and hugged her with all my might. "Eliza! You're about to become a grandmother! What better or more spectacular Christmas gift could you possibly receive?"

I stepped away. Even in the pitch-black dark I could see her smiling through her tears. She waved, blew me a kiss, and said, "Oh my! Ms. Theodora! You're right! Merry Christmas to you, too! Thank you!"

When I returned to the living room, I was to receive the next surprise of Christmas. Barbara was delivering a stammering lecture, and for once, Cleland was almost supporting her.

"We are not used to—or I mean, we are not completely unfamiliar with the insides of a kitchen," she said. "I think, if we all pitch in and do a little, everybody doing something, we can certainly get Christmas Eve and Christmas-day dinner on the table. Right? I mean, why can't we?"

Faces were frozen in trepidation. Paranoid fantasies of food poisoning even crossed *my* mind. What about burns and mad dashes to the emergency room? Did we even *have* an aloe plant? Did we know a plastic surgeon? A good gastroenterologist? There was a weighty silence as everyone considered Barbara's lack of expertise with anything beyond the microwave she engaged for heating leftovers.

"Let's try to be optimistic. Perhaps this Jewel, if she shows up, will know how to cook. Perhaps she will be useful," Cleland said, shrugging his shoulders toward my Barbara. "If not, your mother can make her specialty—peanut butter and jelly sand-wiches." He chuckled at his ridiculous joke. No one else joined in.

Not nice, I thought. I have already confessed that Barbara is not the next incarnation of Julia Child. So what? I decided she could absolutely produce a turkey dinner with all the trimmings if I supervised her and the others kept the floor dry. We could cer-tainly make a simple pasta dish for Christmas Eve, couldn't we? Was it necessary for Cleland to be so sarcastic?

"Well, I can't do dishes," Lynette said. "I just spent forty-something dollars to get these here nails put on."

She held out for inspection her long barber-pole French-manicured fingernails, which, through the wonders of airbrushing or stencils, resembled candy canes. It was a bold remark for Lynette and a vulgar one.

"Lynette? You know what I think about fake nails," George said.

Lynette blushed. Fake *anything* never sat well with George, even though I was certain his hair was tinted. To say nothing of her, ahem, red hair. Try as he might, he would never transform her into a socialite. Here's something else. *Usually* Lynette was the nicest one of the bunch, which should tell you something.

"Hon? You'll wear gloves like those housewives on television and you'll manage," Camille said, as though she had never washed a dish in her life and had no intention of washing one during this holiday, either.

"Excuse me," I said. They all froze and looked at me as though I had stopped by from another planet. "It is almost Christmas Eve. It may well be my last. If anyone cares to know what *I'd* like for Christmas, I wish for once, just for the next two days, that you all would *be nice* to each other. That's all I wish."

There was not one peep from any of them.

"It's not too much to ask, is it?"

Silence begat silence.

"Well then, it's almost nine. I'm going to bed," I said. "If Eliza calls, please wake me. Good night."

I went to each one of them and gave them a little air kiss on the cheek and hugged my great-grandchildren.

I leaned down to the little impertinent Teddie, and with the most serious face I could muster, I said, "If *you* don't believe in Santa, *he* doesn't come. So if I were you, I'd reconsider my position."

Teddie turned red as a beet and spun on her heel toward George, burying herself in his side. George did not utter a syllable in rebuttal. I looked to Camille, Barbara, and Cleland. They appeared slightly chastened. Good!

Not my pudgy little Andrew. He was guilty of nothing! His beautiful chocolate eyes grew wide and he smiled at me.

"Do you believe in Santa?" he said.

"I surely do," I said, squeezing both of his shoulders.

"I love you, Gigi."

Andrew called me Gigi, which stood for great-grandmother.

"I love you, too."

Heaven knows, that child was an absolute angel. How he'd wound up in this family was anybody's guess.

I stood to my full height, which was a fraction less than it had been in prior years, and surveyed them, this small sea of dissatisfied faces bobbing before me like wontons in a bowl of soup, lives of privilege, good health, safety, reasonable intelligence— and what? They didn't have a toothpick of gratitude for all they had been given. I nodded to them and left the room. I left them in silence, and then, to my surprise, I heard Cleland clear his throat and mutter something to George about how I was right! See? He wasn't always a skunk!

It was going on ten o'clock and I was exhausted.

I climbed the stairs and went to my room. After changing into my nightclothes and moisturizing—for the sake of itch not to sustain youth—I got into my bed and kissed the picture of Fred that I kept beside my bed. It was true enough that my grief over losing him was at least partially responsible for the household gloom and I reminded myself to buck up, at least for the sake of the children.

On a brighter note, I loved my room. It was one of six on the safer haven of the second floor. I actually liked it better than the master bedroom. It was less chilly and had a fireplace with a lovely gray-and-white marble mantelpiece. A marginally refurbished bathroom was attached to the room, so that gave me additional privacy. When I traded bedrooms with Barbara and Cleland, I redecorated this room with beautiful yellow jacquard chintz that was covered in pink flowers and green leaves. It was very cheerful, and just being there was like getting a shot of vitamin B_{12}. I had a large comfortable club chair and ottoman near the window that was positioned for beautiful afternoon light for reading. Books were my passion and my escape from the madness.

At the other end of the floor, Cleland and Barbara were ensconced in the room I had once shared with Fred after my parents passed on. I'd sensed that Cleland was just dying to assume the grandest bedroom, so I let them have it, rather than making them wait around for me to go dancing into eternity with the Grim Reaper. I didn't care. I would have done *anything* I could to make Cleland feel like the lord of the manor. I always hoped that those concessions and my financial contributions to the house would make him be a little nicer to my daughter. If I had to hang a title on his general demeanor, I would say that Cleland was *resigned* to his marriage. It was not and never had been a source of great joy for him. So my efforts were probably futile, as you couldn't make someone love and adore somebody when they plainly did not.

Fortunately, the square footage of the house kept us at a pleasant enough distance from one another. The room next to mine was a guest room, which we referred to as the Green Room, even though it had not been green for eons. When they came to visit, George and Lynette stayed in the room opposite it, which was called the Bridal Suite for some reason

I can't recall—probably since it was decorated in hues and patterns of ivory and it housed a beautiful old rock-crystal chandelier. Teddie occupied the room next to them, which was wallpapered in pastel shades of pink and green. It was so feminine and sweet. I sighed thinking how it would be so lovely if these qualities rubbed off on her, but then, she was at a difficult age, poor child. But she was not a stupid child, just inconsiderate and insensitive. I decided I would spend some time with her, if she would let me, and we would talk about life and how to make it beautiful for everyone around you. That was it! I would use every trick in my book to pound a little grace into her.

Cleland used the room next to the master bedroom as his study, which buffered any sounds that might have echoed through the walls from the others' arguing or late-night television, which they turned up when they argued.

Since the end of November, right after Thanksgiving, Camille and Andrew had been staying on the third floor, about which I had increasing concern. I was afraid that it might become a permanent arrangement if she didn't get things sorted out with Grayson, who, to the best of my knowledge, was in Atlanta.

The greatest positive aspect about having them all under one roof for the holiday was the hope that they would perhaps recognize their own foolishness by witnessing it in one another and, somehow, shape up. It was a lot to hope for and I knew it, but it was the last thought I remembered before I fell into a deep sleep.

Then the terrible dreams, the worst nightmares of my entire life began.

I dreamed of Pearl and my grandmother Dora, for whom I was named. I was a little girl and we were all in the kitchen baking cookies for Christmas, just simple sugar cookies. They were the kind you rolled out and cut into shapes—bells, stars, trees, and so forth—with metal cookie cutters. Even in my dreams, I could smell the butter and sugar as they swirled through the air. I would have sworn, except for the fact that ladies don't swear, that the smell was real and that my mouth actually watered. We were all happy. Then Pearl turned to me and she was angry, angrier than I had ever seen her.

"How did you let them turn out to be like this? How? Didn't I teach you better?"

"I'm just a little girl!" I said. "Who are you talking about?"

Now, in my dream I knew I was a grown-up and

that Pearl and my grandmother were dead. I realized but did not want to acknowledge that Pearl was referring to the generations of us that she and my grandmother had left behind to spiral down into a bucket of rattlesnakes. With that thought, rattlesnakes began to crawl from all the pots on the stove until they covered the floor of the kitchen. They threatened and hissed, rising and squirming. I tried to scream. No noise would come from my throat.

In a flash, the hazy light of my dream changed to a midday clarity, and my grandmother disappeared. Pearl and I were in the kitchen alone. The snakes were gone. I was my present age and I knew beyond a doubt that this was no longer a dream. It was a visitation. If you thought the snakes were bad, this was worse. Much worse. Pearl looked at me with those spooky brown-rimmed, hazel eyes of hers and set her jaw like she was going to kill me dead. She exhaled so long and hard I could actually feel the heat of her breath on my arm.

"What is the matter with your family?"

"Please help me, Pearl!"

"Help you? I spent a lifetime helping you!"

"What have I done? Why are you so angry?"

"It is not what you have done, Ms. Theodora! It is what you have *not* done!"

"What can I do now? I'm so old! No one cares what I think! No one!"

She must have realized the truth of what I said. She calmed down a little and was quiet. She said, "Listen up, 'eah? I gots one more t'ing to do to get in dem Pearly Gate and I guess your hard heads be it. I gwine set dem all straight and den I gets my wings. Gawd he'p dem that gets in my way."

For the rest of the night, I lay in my bed with my eyelids glued together, perspiring and shaking all over. I was terrified, listening to the earsplitting wind howling and screeching all around the house. Every window in the house rattled to the point where they should have fallen from their frames. Above and below, the floors creaked from footsteps, even though I knew everyone was in bed, fast asleep for hours. Something from beyond the natural world was coming closer and closer. Crazy as this sounds, I knew it was real as sure as I knew anything. All our ghosts were rising up in protest against us and in support of Pearl. For the thousandth time, I beseeched the Almighty for protection.

It wasn't the noises that were so terrible, it was the vision of Pearl. She was beyond furious with me. In fact, it made me highly nervous.

All at once, the world became as quiet as could be. The only sound I could hear was the rapid beating of my own heart. I reached for my glasses and looked at my alarm clock beside the bed. It was eight o'clock in the morning! Morning had come and I had slept! How was this possible? I was always up by six! I was sure that I would wake up in the kitchen, but I did not. I woke up in my bed and my old heart was slamming against my ribs like a butcher trying to tenderize a bargain cut of steak. Short of breath and pulse racing, I took what seemed like an eternity to calm myself. I wasn't sure if what I remembered was a dream. I concluded that it *must* have been. Either it was a dream or at long last I was losing my marbles. Had the screaming wind been a dream, too? All the rattles and creaks? Or was Pearl *really* angry?

I felt perfectly rested, so I must've slept more soundly than I thought. Something told me I was going to need extra stamina to get through the day.

I crept out from under my covers and gasped as I looked out through the window, astounded. The air was so thick with fog it was as though a stew had rolled in across the harbor. I had not seen such a dense fog cover in the entirety of my days. If it had not been Christmas Eve, it would have been the perfect occasion to crawl right back into bed and sleep the day away. Not that I had ever done that.

I was confused. Very confused. I tried to focus on what there was to be done. I *had* to help Barbara produce a successful holiday. Maybe then Pearl, wherever she was, would forgive my sloth. I could not fail Barbara!

As quickly as I could, I dressed for Christmas Eve in my favorite red knit dress and jacket and attached the same pin I had worn yesterday to the lapel. As I swallowed the arsenal of pills I took each day to keep my wheels turning, I looked at myself in the full-length mirror. I decided that I could pass for eighty any day of the week. Not bad. Just as I was descending the center-hall stairs, the doorbell rang. Barbara answered before I could reach it.

"You must be Jewel! Thank you for coming! Come in! Come in!"

Barbara stepped aside to let this great shadowy figure of a woman carrying a small suitcase pass.

It was Pearl.

Christmas Eve

It was Pearl all right. I began to shake.

She stepped through the blankets of wet heavy mist and squarely onto the black-and-white check-erboard floor of our entrance hall. She scanned her surroundings for a few moments to reac-quaint herself with the house she had known so well decades ago. In slow motion, she lowered her old-fashioned, weathered brown leather valise to rest by her feet. She removed her black knit gloves finger by finger, laid one on top of the other, put-ting them neatly in her handbag. Next, she slipped out of her red wool coat and folded it over her arm. She smiled, giving Barbara a head-to-toe as-sessment and filling the foyer with loving warmth. She was glad to be back, to see who my daughter was. Step one of her mission had begun.

There had never been a life force more powerful than the energy Pearl exuded when she was on a mission. Now she had a *Christmas* mission, her favorite kind.

Barbara shrank back, realizing she was in the presence of an extremely formidable woman. She began to babble, something she did when nervous.

"Merry Christmas—well, *almost*! This is some weather, isn't it? Some fog! Just crazy!" She said, "Thank you for coming! Can I—I mean, do *you*, uh, is there anything I can do to help you get comfortable? I mean, may I show you, you know, around?"

"No'm. Best if I just get to work."

"Yes. Of course! You're right, *of course*. There's so much to do today . . ." Barbara said. "Christmas Eve and all . . ."

"Yes'm. We'll have a nice dinner around one, cocktails at seven, and supper at eight."

"We usually have supper at six . . ." Barbara's voice trailed off to nothingness as Pearl cut her an eye. "But eight's just fine . . . just fine . . ."

"Good. Then that's settled. I'll holler if I need anything."

"Oh! Yes, of course! By all means! I'll be in and out all day, even in this *fog* . . . last minute errands, you know . . . I have to . . . Christmas Eve?"

"Yes'm."

Barbara hurried toward me, passing me on the

stairs, and whispered, "Whew! She's something, isn't she?"

"Uh-huh," I said, trembling all over. Something like a living, breathing, flesh-and-blood *ghost*.

Pearl swung a glance to her right at the Christmas tree and harrumphed loudly. Finally, she looked up at me standing on the landing as if to say, *Well, well! Who's this little old lady? Is this my Theodora?* I must admit that I was still in a frightful state of shock to see her, and I hung on to the rail with both hands so my wobbling legs wouldn't give out from under me. I wondered, was I seeing things? Did she recognize me? Then she smiled from ear to ear.

When she grinned at me, I knew that she did. Undeterred by the fact that a dead person was standing right there as plain as day was day, I grinned right back at her. Mine was an unstable nervous grin, to be sure.

She picked up her suitcase and headed for the kitchen. I took another deep breath to steady myself, then another, and slowly, slowly, I followed her. Gracious! For all I had learned in my years, I was very unfamiliar with dealing with the living dead. What in the world would I do?

By the time I got to the kitchen, as my pace was not as brisk as hers, she was coming out of the spare room with a small bathroom that had historically been reserved for emergency sleepover help or storage. Well, we certainly had reached the point of a spiritual emergency, so I assumed that she would be staying there—if dead people showered or slept, that is.

She was tying a crisp white cotton apron around her neck and waist as though she had never left.

Was she really Pearl? I was almost one hundred percent certain that she was. Still, I had to ask. Knowing that Pearl had never been one to pussy-foot around, I decided there and then to just speak my mind. If I was wrong, she would just think I was a half-witted old lady, I'd go live in the attic, and we would be done with it. I prayed I would be wrong, but knew the outcome before I said a word.

"I know *who* you are," I said, with a profound warble in my voice.

"I know who *you* are, too! Good to lay eyes on you again, but *Lawsamercy!* How *old* are you? Time's flying, ain't it?"

Without missing a beat, I said, "Hmmph!" We always *hmmphed* each other, even when I was a young child. "Well! If your clock hadn't stopped ticking, I think you'd be right around one hundred and thirty-three years old. So who's calling who *old*? Hmm?"

Pearl threw back her head and laughed. Her laugh was so hearty that the sound of its music made me laugh, too. I had missed her mightily and wanted to throw my arms around her. Suspicion held me in my place. After all, this *still* might have been a hallucination! Old people my age had all sorts of dementia and this could have been some sort of psychological episode.

She began opening cabinets, the refrigerator and the freezer, taking inventory.

"Well, I see you can still do your math in your head."

I found myself talking to her despite my strong suspicions. "Useless skill *these* days . . . with computers, calculators, and all that . . ." Then I wanted so badly to believe that help had arrived in the form of the finest—albeit dead—woman I had ever known that my heart gave in to the impossibility of it all. I accepted that it was indeed her. "Oh, *goodness*! It's so *grand* to see you, Pearl."

"What? You think I wasn't coming? What's going on around 'eah?"

When she looked back at me her eyebrows were drawn together in disappointment, or perhaps bewilderment. I wasn't quite sure why.

"Well, who knew if you *could*? Anyway, I can hardly believe my eyes!" I took a handkerchief from my pocket, removed my glasses, and wiped my eyes, which, yes, were tearing. "How did you do this—I mean, get here? Golly! My heart is still pounding like mad! Tell me! How is my Fred? Have you seen him?"

"I got 'eah on the Mercy Train and don't ask me no questions. It's breaking the rules."

"Not even about Gordie? Oh, please, Pearl! My poor brother? My parents? Please tell me they are all right!"

"They are all right. All right? Now, that's all. We gots to get to work!"

She wasn't budging an inch, and I knew it was wrong to ask her to break the rules and cost her a pair of wings, although I had to chuckle a little at the thought of Pearl as an angel or as an emissary of one. Anyway, what was the difference? If she was *here* there had to be others *there*, wherever and whatever *there* was. Evidently, this was all the consolation and information I was to receive. To tell the truth, it was all I needed, and given the messy predicament we were in, it was probably more than I deserved.

"Well," I said, my heartbeat finally returning to almost normal, "I thought I might come give you a hand. You didn't have convection ovens or microwaves in your day, or food processors and so forth."

"Ms. Theodora? No disrespect? Iffin I can get myself down 'eah in the flesh, I reckon I can figure—"

"Sorry! Of course you can! What was I thinking? Would you like some hot tea? I mean, do you eat and drink?"

"Why not?" She continued opening cabinets and canisters and shaking her head.

"What's wrong?"

Pearl exhaled for a long enough stretch to launch a cruise ship and send it straight to the docks in Hamilton, Bermuda.

She said, "Where's the fruitcake?"

"Fruitcake?"

"Yes'm, the fruitcake. And nut cake, rum balls, sands, fondant . . . no cookies?"

"Well, over the years fruitcake has gained a bad reputation, and all those other things are considered unhealthy, you know, loaded with trans fats and refined sugar?" I filled the kettle with water and put it on the burner to boil. My hands were still trembling.

"Hmmph! Like we all didn't live long lives eating what we darn well *felt* like eating! It's about moderation! And *what's* the matter with that Christmas tree out there, and *where* is the manger scene?"

"Horrible, isn't it? This year's tree seems to be an absolute triumph of bad taste over tradition and decorum. Heavens! Don't say *I* said that. Do you mean the crèche set or the manger scene?"

"Both!"

"Oh, me. I'm sorry to say that people don't care about that kind of thing anymore, Pearl. It's so sad. No one seems to want to carry on the old traditions. Well, some do, but not this family."

"Hmmph." She put her hands on her hips. "Is there any blackberry brandy in this 'eah house?"

"Yes, look in the pantry next to the Marsala wine. Why? What are you making?"

Pearl looked at me and smiled so wide it sent a chill up my spine.

"I'm making *Pearl* feel better, and then you and I are making a *plan*."

Pearl poured herself a small glass of brandy, and

I knew at once why she had always smelled like blackberries. Old Pearl liked a little nip.

"This 'eah is the only one thing I miss from this earth."

"Well, help yourself! I'll see to it that there's an endless supply for you!"

"Oh no! Just a little taste is all I want. I hope this ain't breaking the rules."

"Rules against a little glass of something to warm the bones?"

"Hmmph! They rules got rules! 'Sides, I cain't be 'eah too long. Just two days."

"Two days!" I got gooseflesh. "Why only two days?"

"Hmmph. I'm lucky to get two! They only give Cinderella a few hours, 'eah?"

'Eah is a wonderfully versatile old Gullah word that means so many things. It could mean "you hear me?" Or "you come now or else!" Or "isn't it true?"

"Two days? Oh, mercy, Pearl! How will we get them on the right road in such short order?"

"Ms. Theodora? Where's your faith in Pearl?"

I sipped my tea, still not quite believing she was there. There was no denying it; it *was* my Pearl, the same glorious woman who had steered me through the shoals of my childhood. She was the Eighth Wonder of the World, come back to educate my daughter and the generations that had followed. In her own way, she would reveal to them a thing or two about what really mattered in life. She would succeed where I had failed. I looked at my wristwatch.

"Mercy! Pearl! We've hired someone to come and help. A woman named Jewel! What are we to do when she shows up?"

"Don't fret. She ain't coming 'eah. I done seen to that. She forgot. Now you got a pencil and some paper? We need to be making a list. I'll get that ham in the refrigerator going and a pot of red rice. There's what I need for biscuits and I saw some greens soaking . . ."

I had taken a pad and pencil from the drawer and put it in front of her. "The collards?"

"Yeah, I reckon Eliza who works 'eah . . ."

"Eliza? Oh, I haven't told you this . . . I'm so worried about her! Her daughter . . ."

"My darlin'? Don't pay that no never mind! I know all about that situation and it's well in hand. They's fine."

"Praise the Lord!"

"Amen. So, I need a few things from the store, and *wait*! Where's everybody? How come they ain't in 'eah to see what's going on? Where's the Christmas spirit? And that manger scene your daddy had built? He musta spent a fortune on that. They gots to get that out and set up!"

"You know what? You're right! I'll handle this!"

"Good luck!"

"Watch me!" I said. "I'll switch them good if they give me any trouble!"

Pearl laughed and shook her head at my sudden initiative.

I was going to help!

I found Cleland and George, and I can tell you they were not very happy with my request. They stammered and sputtered all around like old Demosthenes, their mouths filled with pebbles. Finally they agreed to do as I had asked. It was not as though I had requested either of them to serve as a living organ donor, after all.

By the time I returned to the kitchen, the ham was miraculously in the oven and the rest of dinner simmered on the stove. The mysteries of Pearl filled the air, as did the mouthwatering aroma of brown sugar crystallizing with mustard and cloves.

I could hear George and Cleland complaining

all the way from where I sat. They grumbled and struggled under the weight and proportions of the plywood pieces of the outdoor manger scene as they carried them down the front-hall stairs. Pearl and I looked at each other and snickered. I got up and left the kitchen for a moment to take a peek. They had located the three sides and the roof of the stable, the figures, and the manger. George and Cleland were leaning against the table in the front hall as though this little bit of effort had completely worn them out.

I felt much worse for the manger itself. The whole shebang had been cooped up in the cynicism of the attic forever and was filthy dirty from doing nothing except getting dustier by the year and growing sticky cobwebs. I quickly closed the door and hoped they hadn't seen me.

"Who you hiding from?" Pearl said.

"Cleland and George."

"How come?"

"They have very bad tempers."

"Hmmph," she said, indicating she thought that was absurd. "That ain't no concern of mine! Shouldn't be no concern of yours neither!"

A minute or two later, Cleland and George appeared in the kitchen to deliver a condition report and the fact that there was no Baby Jesus to be found.

"I don't think it's gonna be worth the effort," Cleland said. "That thing's pretty disgusting. Besides, it's so foggy outside, no one's going to see it."

"Yeah," George said, "what's the point? Christmas is tomorrow. Seems like a lot of effort for just one day. 'Sides, there ain't no Jesus."

Pearl narrowed her eyes at them as though George had made the statement as a religious conviction. With a dour, and I mean *dour,* expression, she reached in the pantry closet, handed them two rolls of paper towels and two bottles of a spray cleaner.

"Ain't got no baby 'cause He ain't come yet. So, iffin y'all think this 'eah job is too hard, or that it ain't worth the trouble, just let me know."

They skulked away in a combination of anger and unfamiliar mortification, saying something about assigning the cleaning job to Andrew to help him lose some baby fat.

"He could use the exercise," Cleland said with a snort.

"I gots plans for Andrew!" Pearl said.

George, unaccustomed to being bossed around, especially by a woman, opened his ugly mouth. "We'll send him *skirt side* when he gets home. *He's gone shopping at the mall with his granny and his mommy.*"

George's high-pitched nasal tone implied that Andrew was a sissy. I didn't like it one bit.

"He's just a little boy," I said, empowered by Pearl's presence to register my discontent.

Pearl arched her eyebrow in disapproval. They saw it.

"He's probably going to shake them down for some candy. Or a last-minute toy."

Holy cow! *Cleland* had made a halfhearted attempt to render an awkward moment less tense.

"Probably," George conceded.

Pearl looked George up and down with what we used to call the *hairy eyeball* and I could sense George's discomfort.

"That's how you speak of your only nephew on Christmas Eve? Or on any eve for that matter? That's not nice."

"Oh, I was just kidding," George said. "Can't you take a joke?"

"Hmmph. You call that a *joke?* Whatever you say. Anyway, they went shopping for me for *y'all's* supper, too. When they come back, send that child in 'eah to me, and his cousin Teddie, too! And Camille!"

In the span of one morning, the arrival of Pearl had put sarcasm and laziness on a short leash. Verbally spanked and without any further objection, the men went to set up the manger in the front yard.

Pearl took out a large mixing bowl. She snapped her fingers and it was filled with fruitcake batter. *What?* I couldn't believe it! I took off my glasses, rubbed my eyes once again, and stared hard at the batter in the bowl. It was there, all right. There was simply no explaining it.

"What you think? I ain't got all day to be chopping nuts and messing with all this sticky fruit," she said. "We gots bigger heads to knock!"

My eyes were about to grow wider.

She took out a smaller mixing bowl and snapped her fingers again. In an instant it was filled with the mixture for sands.

"This is just . . . you are amazing," I said, with a definite gasp.

"Fuh true!" She winked at me. "We ain't got one minute to waste. Remember how long this used to take us? Lawsa! We woulda been chopping nuts for two months!"

She pointed to a third bowl and it was quickly filled with all the ingredients for rum balls. She covered them all with dish towels, tied the towels around the rim of the bowls with string, and placed them in the refrigerator.

This time I put my hand to my chest to be sure my heart was still functioning. Surprisingly, it was. Why had I expected anything less? I was actually becoming accustomed to Pearl's paranormal display and, I'd admit, I was thoroughly amused. Although still extremely curious. It was just like watching a magician pull rabbits from a hat or make people disappear—it didn't seem possible! Face it, Theodora, I told myself, everything normal had been left at the door when Pearl walked in!

"May I ask how, just *how,* you did that?"

Pearl looked up to the ceiling, folded her hands, and smiled in total innocence. "With a little help from my angelic friends."

"Hmm. It's reassuring to know there *are* angelic friends to be had." Pearl squinted at me like she was using X-ray vision to see if I had pagan blood flowing in my veins to even question such a thing. I cleared my throat and continued: "No, no! I believe! I believe!"

"Hmmph! You had better!"

"Hmmph, yourself! By the way, nowadays we

have a plastic wrap that can seal bowls tightly. It's in the drawer over there."

Pearl opened the drawer and saw boxes of plastic bags in three sizes, a box of plastic wrap, and another of aluminum foil.

"Well, would you looky 'eah?" She pulled a long sheet of plastic wrap, tried to sever it on the serrated edge of the box, and of course it stuck to itself and became entangled into a plastic wad. "Hmmph. Waste of good money iffin you ask me!"

"Oh! My dear friend, there are so many things that are a waste of time and money in today's world, it would make your head spin."

"I reckon that's fuh true, too!"

"You can't believe how people live! Start with that blasted huge television back there in the family room! It's high-def, whatever *that* is! The drone of it is absolutely stupefying. When the adults aren't staring at some violence beyond description on the thing, the young people are playing video games, which are like a narcotic designed to make you into an idiot, if you ask me . . ."

I went on and on with my personal diatribe against the modern world and how it all but shunned board games, jigsaw puzzles, and other old-fashioned pastimes. These things brought families together in favor of all the solitary pursuits that didn't enrich anyone's life by one iota, and worse, these mindless, worthless activities kept families apart. Pearl agreed with me about it all.

Except she said, "I guess you have to wonder who allows all this foolishness to go on?"

"You're right," I said. "Barbara and Cleland should've put their foot down."

"Iffin they ain't gwine do it, who then?"

"Me?"

"Hmmph. It ain't fuh me to be the judge."

We talked for a long time as we drank cup after cup of tea, each of Pearl's of course laced with a tiny shot of blackberry brandy. Although we were in the kitchen, we seemed to have been barricaded in our own space and time so that we could talk uninterrupted about all the heavy stones I carried.

"They don't even like to read!"

"What? Lawsamercy! Now, whose fault is that? That is a sin fuh sure!"

"You're right." I sighed hard. "I see it now. You're absolutely right. I should have read to Barbara more when she was little."

She stared at me with a crooked knowing smile. She had me nailed to the wall again. But Barbara

had become apathetic and simply shirked her re-
sponsibilities. No! That wasn't right. Barbara
floundered because of my failure to give her a clear
and concise direction. I had never adjusted to life
without Fred, and in some ways was just sitting
around waiting to die. I felt terrible that I had been
so self-absorbed.

She patted the back of my hand and sniffed the
air. "Don't fret so. That's why I'm 'eah, and guess
what? That ham's done!"

I felt my spirits rise a little, but oh, my soul was
still deeply troubled.

Pearl lifted the fruited and glazed ham from the
oven and placed it on the counter. I cannot tell you
how divine it looked. There was nothing else in the
world that mattered except that ham! It could have
been on the cover of a magazine! I could barely
muster the discipline to restrain myself from slicing
a little piece off its bone right that second.

The red rice was steaming away, and the combined fragrance of bacon, onions, and tomatoes
was fueling the flames of an appetite I had not
known in decades. What was happening? The
collards smelled—well, they smelled like collards
smell. Rank. Pearl knew what to do. She threw a
long dash of vinegar in the water to squelch the

stench. I would be tortured by *famine* until lunch was on the table.

She raised the oven temperature, dusted the marble slab with flour, and I knew she was going to make biscuits. The halfhearted but very necessary renovation of the kitchen three years ago had included recycling my mother's pastry slab into the countertop, and from the moment the new kitchen was unveiled, it had remained unused. Good as Eliza was, her biscuits came from a tube in the dairy section of the grocery store. My family seldom ate carbohydrates. The slab would be ceremoniously rechristened by the hands of Pearl.

"There are some things I think I'd like to do myself," she said. "Feels good to have my hands in the dough."

Using her fingers, she crumbled the cold butter into the flour with a dash of salt, and when it looked like gravel, she made a well and poured in cream. As though she was preparing clay for a sculpture, she worked it all together, flopping it over and kneading it several times.

"Why don't I set the table," I said. I'll admit I was thinking more about the rumble in my stomach than the desire to be helpful. "You make the manna."

Pearl giggled, arched one eyebrow, snapped her fingers over her head (a little bit of dough flew in space and disappeared), and she said, "Done! Table's set! You sit and talk to me! Carrying dishes ain't the best use of your time. So, tell your Pearl everything else what's on your mind, Ms. Theodora."

I sighed, loving her more than ever. How long had it been since anyone really cared what I thought about, worried about, or desired? On occasion, Eliza and Barbara did.

"Well, you have seen for yourself, haven't you? I am heartsick about my family. First, there's Barbara and Cleland. I don't know what really goes on between them, but they surely don't seem happy. Barbara is as sweet as pie, but maybe the problem is that she doesn't take *command*. A stronger stance. With *all* of them. The mother has to be the mother to the *whole* family, not stand by while they all ride roughshod over each other. Don't you think?"

"Yes, I do. Haven't you told her that?"

"Well, not exactly, but I have surely indicated it! Gosh, Barbara seems so afraid that, I don't know . . . who knows? Maybe she thinks Cleland might run off and leave her or something . . ."

"No man evah done leave a good woman when

he gots a reason to stay. She gots to give him reasons to stay, 'eah?"

"You're right, of course. You know me. I always think he married her for her money."

"Hmmph. Maybe true, maybe not. He's still here, though, and that don't mean she cain't be spinning a spell to show him why he *should* love her, does it?"

"His career at the bank never amounted to much . . ."

"Well, you know men. They judge they own success by they family, they money, and how they friends see them as manly. Iffin he ain't earning what he thinks he should and his wife be a little dormouse, then how's he supposed to look in the mirror and think much of what he see?"

"No. That's right. He can't." I took another sip of my tea and watched Pearl's hands as she shaped the biscuits into perfect mounds. She was a marvel! "He's just so sarcastic with her. It's so disrespectful, especially when it's in front of me."

"He's only like that because she lets him get away with it. You know, you could tell him to hush his mouth, too."

"I'm not getting in the middle of my daughter's

marriage. She's so depressed I don't even think she knows she's depressed."

"So are you!"

"By golly, Pearl, you're right! I'm depressed and so is she! And you're right again! She *allows* him to behave the way he does! I'm going to speak to her before this day is out."

"So that's one thing. Now, what else we got to do?"

"There's George and Lynette and that—heaven help me . . ."

"That's why I'm 'eah!"

"Right! I mean, forgive me for the thoughts I have about that child of theirs. Now, George is a handsome devil . . ."

"Yes'm, he looks like Cary Grant!"

"He does but he's terrible. He's competitive with everyone, and he's judgmental . . ."

"His Lynette needs to be growing some backbone . . ."

"Absolutely! Then there's Camille and Grayson and their precious Andrew . . ."

I told Pearl all about how they treated one another, but of course she already knew every detail of the whole saga anyway. I guessed she just wanted to hear it from me. Still, she sighed and shook her head.

"Ain't right. But don't you worry."

She ladled the rice and collards into two covered dishes, sliced the ham, placed it on a meat platter, put the fruitcake in a bain-marie and into the oven on low heat. The biscuits were almost ~~too~~ hot to handle. Still, she wrapped them in a linen cloth and put them in a beautiful sweetgrass basket.

The crushing urge to taste one overwhelmed me and I said, "May I?"

"Of course! 'Eah!"

"Thank you!" I couldn't get it into my mouth fast enough! Where did my appetite come from? I was as hungry as a teenage boy! "Oh, Pearl!"

"Light as a feather from a cherub's wing, huh?" She looked up to the ceiling with her hands folded in prayer; a little feather fell from the thin air and I giggled like a schoolgirl.

"Hmmph," she said, "this situation ain't funny!" Despite the truth of her observation, she giggled, too. "Now, that cake gwine take two to three hours," she said, and changed into a fresh apron.

"Do you want me to call them to the table?"

"No'm."

"Pearl? You don't have to say no'm or yes'm or ma'am to me. No one does that anymore, either."

"Ms. Theodora? You can keep your plastic wrap, your television, and your microwave oven and I'll just keep my manners, 'eah? Besides, in the 'eah and now, I'm fabulous and forty-seven and you be my elder. By a lot! 'Eah?"

We laughed so hard at that! I couldn't remember the last time I had laughed such a robust laugh!

She slapped her warm hand on top of my cold one and said, "I'm going to call *Ms. Barbara* to tell the others to get their fannies to the table but quick!"

Oh, my word! Pearl was so mind-boggling, and even though it was logically and physically impossible that she was there with me, with us, she *was*. I wondered again how she would bring about the transformation we all needed and then I remembered what she had said about getting here in the first place . . . Maybe dinner would help things along.

I reminded myself to have faith.

There was a lot to be said about Pearl's cooking. First of all, it had greatly improved since she died. This became evident once we were all seated in our

accustomed places and an off-the-cuff, disingenu-
ous, slap-hazard, perfunctory, record-breaking
blessing for our food had been offered by Cleland.
Usually as rambunctious as a bunch of pirates, the
dining-room table was as silent as could be as everyone devoured—I mean *devoured* like a pack of
wild starving wolves—what Pearl had prepared.

Unfortunately, as soon as lunch was over, the
spell was broken. Pearl came into the dining room
to clear the plates.

"What's that smell, Jewel?" George said, leaning
back in his chair.

"Pearl," Pearl said sweetly. "Fruitcake."

"You're going to break the legs of that chair,
son," Barbara said, and as you might expect, she
was ignored.

"Fruitcake! Oh no! I *hate* fruitcake!" Cleland
said with a juvenile scowl, opening the door for
further dissent to fly right in on the wind.

"I thought Eliza said your name was Jewel,"
Barbara said.

"I reckon Eliza got her gems confused," Pearl
said.

"Fruitcake's *nasty*," George said.

"You don't have to eat it, then, George," I said.

"But we'll see what we see when it's all done." My money, the smart money, was on Pearl.

"By and by, you gwine come to love my fruitcake," Pearl said, smiling at George and Cleland. "Then you gwine miss it when it's gone, 'eah?"

Little Teddie exchanged looks of horror and disgust with her father, George, and threw in more than a few escalating gagging sounds for emphasis.

Lynette held her fingers up to her lips and said in nearly a whisper, "Shush now. That's not nice."

"Oh, sorry! Like you come from a family of *aristocrats*? Leave her alone," George said, and snarled, looking to Camille for support. "Hicks." Even Camille, with that acid-dripping viper's tongue of hers, knew better, and she looked away.

What was the matter with him? Insulting Lynette in front of everyone? On Christmas Eve? George had gone too far.

It seemed that no one was terribly bothered by George's rudeness except me and you know who. Pearl, still moving about in the room but disbelieving her ears, stopped dead in her tracks. I looked at Barbara and waited for her to say something. She cleared her throat.

"That wasn't very nice, George," Barbara said.

Her words held all the power of someone trying to kill a grizzly bear with a broom straw. She didn't even ruffle one of George's feathers.

I stood up. "It was inexcusably rude. Apologize at once."

George gave me an icy dismissive glare and then he cocked his head to one side, stared at Lynette, and said nothing. Lynette burst into tears and ran from the table.

"You children come with me," I said.

Obediently, Teddie and Andrew followed Pearl and me to the kitchen without a word.

"Wash your hands," Pearl said, marching them to the smaller sink.

They did as she asked without one objection and I thought just *that* was a small miracle in and of itself. I mean, when you had him alone, Andrew almost always did as he was told, but sometimes when he and Teddie were in cahoots, he could try to wiggle out of a chore. He was a regulation boy. Teddie's face was flushed and I realized for the first time that she was embarrassed by her father. She was growing up.

"Now, sit up there on them stools and get ready to help roll sands," Pearl said to them, placing the bowl of mixture and a cookie sheet in front of them.

"I'll show you how to make them," I said. "They're like fingers. We used to call them moldy mice!"

"Ew! Gross!" Teddie said, wiggling down from the stool. "Yuck! I'm going to go watch TV."

Andrew, who had pinched off a piece of dough and was munching away on it, said to Teddie, "It's good. Try it!"

"You stay put, missy," Pearl said, and seeing that she meant business, Teddie slowly climbed back to her place. Teddie had some terrible problems with authority figures, but that wasn't the issue then. I thought that perhaps she wanted to escape in order to suffer the indignities of her father's behavior in private or by losing herself in a television program.

"Thank you, sir!" Pearl said to Andrew, and smiled.

Teddie ate a crumb, then a larger bit, shrugged her shoulders, and said, "It's not great but it's not terrible. Sorta reminds me of cookie-dough ice cream. Just how long is this going to take?"

"Till we're done," Pearl said.

Teddie sucked her teeth and made a noise that sounded like *snick*. "Now, how do I do this?"

"Like this," I said, smiling. We had a small win at last. I took a tablespoonful of dough, rolled it between my palms, tidied up the ends, and laid it on the cookie sheet. I handed them each a tablespoon and said, "Now, let's get busy!"

"Andrew picked his nose," Teddie said, and giggled.

"Did not!"

"Did. I saw you."

"Stop your nonsense, Teddie, this is Christmas!" I said. "Andrew? You are only allowed to engage in those activities outside of the house!"

Andrew and Teddie laughed at that and I smiled at them.

Looking up to the ceiling for patience, Pearl scraped the dishes, put them in the sink, and turned on the spigot to cover them with hot sudsy water. Moments later, Camille came in with the remains of the dirty flatware and opened the dishwasher.

"Just throw the plates in here," she said to Pearl.

"No good for the gold trim," Pearl said.

"Oh, who cares?" Camille said. "Buy new."

Barbara came through the swinging door with an armload of goblets and heard what Camille said.

"Pearl's right," I heard myself say. "Anyway, you

can't buy new. That china belonged to my mother. Isn't that so, Barbara?"

Oh, please stand up for this one small cause of preservation, I thought.

"Well, actually, Camille, they *did* belong to my grandmother. Aren't they pretty?"

"Yes, they really are," she said, and looked at the apple green border, pin-striped and edged in gold leaf, as though she were seeing it for the first time. "Just FYI, George's upstairs hollering his head off at Lynette."

"FYI?" Pearl said.

"It's an abbreviation meaning 'for your information' . . . do you want me to go have a word with George and Lynette?" I said. "See if I can help them cool off?"

"No," Barbara said, to my surprise. "I imagine that's my job." Then her self-doubt and hand-wringing returned. She said, "Actually, Cleland can make him behave better than I . . ."

Pearl shot me a look. The moment for my maternal lecture had arrived.

I lifted my chin, stared at Barbara directly in the eye, and said, "I think *you* should be the one who runs this house and sets the tone. Cleland has a bank to run and *you're* supposed to be in charge *here*."

Barbara looked from me to Camille.

"Lots of luck, Mom. They'll never change. He's just mean because he can be, and she takes it because she's afraid of him. Sick," Camille said, and took a bite of the dough. "Hey! This is fabulous! Y'all need help?" She went to the sink and washed her hands.

Camille was right, or at least it seemed to be a plausible explanation.

"Well, it's almost Christmas and stranger things have happened," Pearl said, referring to the surprise of Camille pitching in. "Go show them who's the boss, Ms. Barbara, and don't take no gruff from them."

"Well, I'll try. Dinner was delicious, Pearl. Thank you."

"You are entirely welcome," Pearl said.

Minutes later, the noise overhead became louder. Next we heard Barbara yelling from afar, then Cleland. Doors were slamming, feet were stomping, and it went on and on. It was very upsetting for all of us. Except Pearl, who had a cool demeanor.

"Why can't they just get along?" I said to no one in particular.

"I hate it when they fight," Teddie said, and a

sudden flood of hot tears streamed down her scarlet cheeks. "I just hate it. It makes me so mad."

Perhaps the fact that her parents fought all the time was at the root of Teddie's poor behavior. I had not given it much thought until then. It was true that she was constantly being manipulated to choose her father's affection over her mother's.

Out of the mouth of Andrew came, "Maybe they don't know how to." We all looked at him and he added, "Get along, that is."

Camille looked up and smiled at Andrew and her love for him was apparent to Teddie, who seemed to sulk as she noticed it. She was jealous. I did not blame her. That child needed some affection, and heaven knew, she needed a lot of guidance.

I took a tissue from my pocket and wiped Teddie's face. "Come on, sweetheart. Let's not cry." I felt enormous sympathy for the poor little wretch.

"Well, maybe we're gonna *teach* them how to behave, Teddie," Pearl said. She reached over and rubbed Teddie's back. "It's all gwine be fine, honey. Don't you worry."

"I sure wish *somebody* could," she said, and she stopped crying. "I wish I could believe you."

I felt deeply sorry for the child. She was certainly

entitled to a peaceful home. They had no real problems that I knew of except for George's bullying and churlish ways.

Wait! I had almost overlooked the obvious! We were in the kitchen doing something *together* and it was a start. In fact, it was a *marvelous* new beginning!

Dozens of sands were baked and rum balls were rolled. Toward the end of it all, the children understandably became antsy and we told them they could scamper off. Then the shopping bug bit Camille. She excused herself on the pretense that she had to pick up a last minute gift.

However, before our kitchen party broke up, the children agreed that the sands were the best things they had *ever* eaten. As soon as the first batch was baked to a perfect golden brown and had cooled, Pearl rolled two in powdered sugar and gave them to the children with a glass of milk. They were just delighted.

"You can eat all the ones that break," Pearl said.

"Let's break some," Teddie said. We knew she was only teasing.

"Don't you dare!" Pearl said, taking the threat as a compliment.

Unfortunately, the wariness in Camille lived on, as she batted her eyelashes again and again in disbelief when Andrew and Teddie gave Pearl a firm hug around her waist.

"Be careful driving around in that fog," I said to Camille.

"Don't worry! I'm too young to die!"

"Don't go tempting fate," Pearl said.

Pearl's face was grim as she spoke those words and Camille shuddered.

"I won't," Camille said.

Finally, when there was only Pearl and me left in the kitchen, I said to her, "Tough bunch, huh? Camille likes to take pills and go shopping. With vigor."

"Gotcha. Heaven help us! I may have to resort to a little Gullah magic, too," Pearl said. "I wonder if that would be breaking the daggum rules?" A few seconds later, a light came into her eyes as though she had remembered something. "Hmmph. Watch and see. It's gonna get worse before it gets better."

"What can I do to help?"

"Get that list. Call somebody back in here and send them to the grocery store for me. I need two quarts of pomegranate juice, a quart of orange juice, three dozen eggs, two quarts of heavy whipping cream, and a box of powdered sugar. And fresh nutmegs."

I wrote everything down as quickly as I could. I looked at my scribble in frustration and wondered how in the world anyone else would read it since I could not.

"Pearl?"

"Oh, don't worry yourself so!"

One snap of her fingers and my script became legible. I glared at it in surprise and Pearl laughed so hard she had to lean over and slap her thighs.

"How in the world do you . . . ?"

"Being dead does have *some* advantages!"

"Well, that's nice to know. I mean, I *guess* . . . "

"Oh, hand me the list and *I'll* get them going!"

She snatched the paper from me and disappeared through the swinging door. I turned around, thinking I would put away the food we had made and try to finish the dishes, only to marvel that everything was as clean as it had ever been. Pearl must have snapped her fingers on the way out the door. All the sands were fanned out in layers on a cake plate, the rum balls were piled high in a glistening cut-glass bowl, and the fruitcake, baked to perfection ahead of schedule, rested on a cake rack, filling the air with the exact same divine perfumes I remembered from my childhood.

Of all the five senses, the experts say that smell is the most powerful. For me it was certainly true. My good friend Pearl, on the other hand, seemed to be in possession of a variety of senses. At least six. With her sixth sense and her pockets bulging with every kind of Gullah magic, she was determined that her visit would create a loving order, or else. I didn't want to think about the *or else*. If she succeeded, that loving order would force my family to rise from their acrimonious pit of discord. I hoped. Oh, how I hoped!

What did she want with all that pomegranate juice? I was to find out by six o'clock that evening.

Pearl must have blistered her fingers snapping them that afternoon because family treasures began appearing that we had not seen in years. She resurrected my mother's large punch bowl from somewhere and polished it until you could see your reflection in its sides. My mother's mother had owned a perfectly magnificent ladle that Pearl coaxed into duty from the dark corners of a silver chest and buffed until it was worthy of a queen's table. She placed them both on a gleaming silver rectangular tray whose provenance I could not recall, but knew that I had not seen in at least thirty years. I remembered that it had once belonged to a Charleston family whose ancestor had signed the Declaration of Independence. What could have been more fitting for the moment? This was certain to be a Christmas Eve of historic significance.

Pearl surrounded the bowl with the very same collection of mismatched engraved julep cups we had used for one of Barbara's bridal lunches so many years ago. And for so many other occasions when times were happier and things were different.

I have to say, by then I was somewhat hopeful about success because there was tangible evidence of a shift in the atmosphere. The outdoor manger scene was set up, and to my surprise, everyone made a positive remark about it, even though it tilted to one side. Perhaps more importantly, the children and even Camille, whether they would admit it or not, had found some authentic holiday joy at one another's side while they baked together. And I had gained some insight into Teddie.

Once again, the family relics rested on the dining-room sideboard with the sands, rum balls, and fruit-cake. It did my heart good to see at least some piece of our family's traditions restored. Getting back to the larger problem at hand, holiday food and old relics were nice, but I suspected it was the contents of the punch bowl that would matter.

We were gathered together in the living room, placing last-minute gifts under the tree, listening to a medley of carols played by the Canadian Brass. Although the mood seemed festive, I was nervous, fretting about what the night would bring. Pearl must have read my mind because she brought me my cocktail on the same precious tray Eliza used. She gave me a wink and then turned to the others.

"Y'all want to try some punch? It's an old Gullah recipe my mother used to make for special occasions. It's good, 'eah?"

"Sure," Barbara said. "Can the kids drink it? I mean, is it fortified with spirits?"

Pearl burst into laughter.

"Ms. Barbara?" She laughed again. "It's perfectly safe for the children to drink. In fact, the more everyone drinks the better!"

Pearl could barely contain her unmitigated glee. I knew why she was in stitches. That punch was fortified by spirits, all right, but not spirits of this world.

"Probably better with some rum," Cleland said, and took the bottle from the bar to his place at the table.

"That's up to you, Mr. Cleland," Pearl said.

I followed Pearl back to the kitchen.

"What kind of concoction is in that bowl?"

"We called it the Clean Slate punch."

"What do you mean?"

"I mean, this 'eah family needs to wipe the slate clean. If I was you, I'd stick to bourbon or ice water. Somebody might have to be the referee."

Mystified by her explanation, I went to the dining room, where everyone waited. Teddie and George were the first ones to try it. It didn't appear to have any special effect on them. Soon the others all had a cup and then another. Camille, given to excesses of all kinds, seemed to be serving herself more than double what the others consumed.

"This is so delicious!" she said.

I stuck with my cocktail and sipped it more slowly than I had sipped a drink in twenty years. Maybe longer. All I could do was worry about what was to happen.

Soon we were gathered at the supper table for she-crab soup, which would be followed by bowls of shrimp creole over white rice. We'd always had seafood for Christmas Eve dinner, and even though the children were not particularly fond of it, that night they did not balk or complain. Large baskets of Pearl's light-as-air biscuits almost floated around the table on their own and more punch was served in lieu of water or wine.

However insincere it may have appeared to the outside observer, Cleland offered one of his feeble blessings, and we toasted the holiday and one another. I lifted my spoon and the meal began. At first the conversation was benign enough, but soon I noticed that Camille had developed a little twitch. That bothered me and I hoped to steer the conversation toward a safe harbor.

"What do you want Santa to bring you, Teddie?" I asked, hoping she wouldn't blow the night for Andrew.

"Clothes and stuff. I'm too old for toys."

"I'm not," Andrew said.

"And pierced earrings," Teddie added.

"You're too young for pierced ears," Lynette said. Kindly note that Lynette had at least four holes in each ear.

"No, I'm not!"

"Well, your father thinks so," Lynette said.

"It's not necessary to stick holes in your ears," George said. "What's next? A tattoo?"

Bomb number one was to launch immediately.

"Well, it sure won't say *I heart Dad*," Camille said.

Teddie put her spoon down as her face fell. Frankly, I didn't see why George felt that way about Teddie piercing her ears, but perhaps it was an attempt to delay her maturation in some way. Camille's remark—well, I decided I must have misunderstood what she meant and I took the lead again.

"What are you hoping for, Andrew?" I said.

"A mountain bike. All my friends have them."

The next little bomb dropped.

"If all your friends jumped off the Cooper River Bridge, would you jump, too?" This imbecilic, and hostile, cliché tumbled from the lips of who else? George!

"No, of course not," Andrew replied. His brow wrinkled and he looked down at his lap, frowning, knowing that Christmas Eve or not, he was in unfriendly territory.

"Well, you could sure use the exercise," Teddie said, and snickered. No one joined her. She blanched in embarrassment, but wasn't she simply following her father's lead?

"Know what? You're a creep," Camille said to

George. "Will your schadenfreude cup never be filled? It's bad enough that your little girl is . . . uh, uh, *sadistic*. Given who you are, it should come as no surprise to anyone that you are, too."

Stunned, George clamped his mouth shut. Luckily, the remark flew right over Teddie's head, or surely she would have started screaming to find herself called *sadistic*. And Lord! Schadenfreude? Did George really find delight in the pain of others? I had not heard that term in years! Perish that thought right to a waste bin!

"Would anyone care for more punch?" I said.

"Sure, Gran, thanks," Camille said. "While we're on the topic of stinkers . . . Daddy? I saw you at lunch today at Peninsula Grill."

Cleland stammered around and finally said, "I was having a business lunch."

"Sure. Monkey business."

Barbara looked up at Cleland and then said to Camille, "Maybe we should talk about your daddy's business *friends* another time. I think I would like some more punch. Will you get it for me, dear?" She held her cup out toward George.

"Sure," he said, and got up. "Maybe one reason Dad has *friends* is that you act like the imperious queen of an ice castle."

"I don't think this is nice talk for Christmas Eve, George," I said.

"It's okay," Cleland said. "I married her for her castle and she doesn't care."

Barbara's face turned crimson and her eyes filled with tears.

"Cleland, I know what you do and where you go. It doesn't matter. I have always loved you. I wish I could make you feel differently about me. And, I wish you would drink a little less."

"You're a fine one to talk," Cleland said with a scowl.

"I'd drink, too, if I had a philandering husband," Lynette said in a screwball defense of Barbara.

"You do have one," Camille said, throwing another hand grenade into the evening.

"Oh, shut up, Camille. Why don't you take your pill-popping bahunkus shopping and spend some *more* money!" George said.

"The stores are closed," Lynette said.

"There's always another day," Camille said.

In the brain, off the tongue. I was terrified. I also realized if this punch was forcing them all to tell the raw naked truth, it appeared that only Barbara and Andrew had nothing to hide.

"Are you running around on me, George?" Lynette asked.

"I'm a man, aren't I?" George turned to Cleland. "I learned it all from you, Pops. It took me three marriages and watching how indifferently you treat Mom to figure this out. You don't have to love women for them to give you babies."

"Really?" Lynette said.

"Yeah, *really*!" George said.

"You're a disgrace and a coldhearted . . . I won't use the word with the ladies present," Cleland said to George. "But I think you know what I mean. Do you know what an embarrassment you are?"

"Me? Me a disgrace? I make five times the money you do! What have you ever accomplished in your life?"

Lynette stood up. "You don't love me, George? Well, I've got news for you, Georgie. Merry Christmas! Teddie ain't yours!"

"What? What? Daddy's not my daddy?" Teddie started kicking the table and everything rattled and rattled.

The wind picked up, howling as it had last evening, and it seemed to me that the walls were undulating in anger and disgust.

"It doesn't matter if he's your biological daddy, hon," Camille said. "You're just like him anyway."

"Yeah? Well, my daddy says the reason Andrew doesn't have a daddy is that you're a man-hater. Uncle Grayson left you because you wouldn't stop shopping! And the reason Andrew is so stupid is because you're on drugs all the time."

"My mama is *not* on drugs and I am *not* stupid!" Andrew said, bursting into a geyser of very impressive tears. "How do you think life is for me? I can build the Chrysler building out of a box of legos, but I can't read the directions right to build a simple fort! Then, in class . . . kids laugh at me when it's my turn to read, but I can recite almost word for word what I hear . . . sometimes I think I want to just die. Just die."

"You don't mean that, Andrew," Camille said. "Please don't say that."

"Moron! Moron! Fat little moron!" Teddie said in a most obnoxious singsong.

"Shut up!" Camille said.

Lynette grabbed Teddie's arm to quiet her. I began to panic. What in the world was happening? This was terrible! They were saying such loathsome things that they would never forgive one another! Pearl was absolutely wrong. *Absolutely wrong!*

With the toe of my shoe I pressed the buzzer under the rug at my place to bring her from the kitchen. Barbara had a buzzer, too, but perhaps she was too upset to use it. On top of it all, the windows were beginning to rattle, and I swanny to heaven, I thought this time they would shatter and come crashing to the floor for certain!

"Aren't we a lovely family?" Camille said. She turned to Teddie. "Let me tell you something, you sassy little urchin of unknown origins, my son Andrew is not a moron. You are. And my husband never left me over money."

Where was Pearl?

"I think . . ." I said.

"What?" they all said at once.

"I think y'all better stop all this hateful talk, right this very second, or you all will regret it later."

Pearl appeared, and as you might guess, she snapped her fingers in the air. A sudden silence occurred. Everyone seemed to lose their voices and the desire to fight. Except for Barbara and Andrew, my family had once again proven that they were an odious lot. Were they in some hypnotic state? Undoubtedly! Was this progress? I didn't think so.

Pearl placed a tureen on the sideboard and took

away everyone's soup plates. She returned and began to ladle out the she-crab soup.

"How's it going?" she whispered to me when she came to my side.

"You know perfectly well . . . Pearl? *What* are you doing? This is the *worst* Christmas of my *entire* life. Please! Make this stop!"

I was hopping mad. Worse, although Pearl knew how angry I was, she had the gumption to smile at me. Worse still, she placed a box of tissues at both ends of the dining-room table because Barbara, Andrew, Teddie, Camille, and Lynette were all weeping in silence. George and Cleland's faces were filled with alarm and consternation and I was on the edge of a crying jag myself. It was just too much. Every picture in the room went askew, and even in my peripheral vision, I could see that the Christmas tree lights had gone haywire, blinking at triple their usual speed.

"Hold steady," Pearl said.

When she had served the last plate and refilled the cups with punch, she left the room. Everyone began to talk and eat, but it seemed they were in a trance.

"This is the best she-crab soup I have ever had in my life," Barbara said.

"It is," Cleland said.

"Yes," the rest of them said.

It *was* absolutely delectable, but who cared about soup at that moment? I looked from face to face. Tears were flowing from the women and children, but they were eating so fast you would have thought it was their first meal in months. The men seemed to have been stricken with a kind of dark-eyed lockjaw but they were eating, too, as though they were completely famished.

There was no doubt about it; the punch had delivered them to some kind of altered state of mind. All their sins and secrets, or at least I *hoped* all their sins and secrets, were laid out in front of them.

Pearl reappeared and cleared the table. Silently she sliced the fruitcake onto dessert plates and added two rum balls, a sand, and a dollop of whipping cream to each portion.

When their dessert plates were empty, which was almost instantaneously, my family members began to rise, yawning and yawning, one by one. Cleland left the room, saying nothing. Barbara followed. Camille took Andrew by the hand; he grabbed a rum ball, fed it to her, and took one for himself. George looked warily at Lynette and then to Teddie. His bitterness seemed to melt like butter on a hot skillet. His expression turned blank as he yawned, his jaw dropping open to a size that could have swallowed Jonah *and* the whale. He put his arm around Lynette and took Teddie's hand into his. Suddenly I was alone at the table.

I looked at my wristwatch. It was midnight! Where had the time gone? I pressed the buzzer under my toe again.

Pearl appeared out of nowhere with the small silver tray. On it was a small glass of blackberry brandy and another mint julep. I took my glass and she lifted hers.

"It's Christmas, Ms. Theodora! Merry Christmas!"

"Are you *sure* about that?" I said. "Is it merry?"

"As sure as I have ever been about anything in my life or after . . ."

I had serious doubts.

Part Three

· CHRISTMAS DAY ·

I knew it was Christmas morning as the warm first light of day washed across the foot of my bed. Something was different; I mean beyond Pearl's presence and all the accompanying drama. The normal sounds of early day were muffled. It was unusually quiet.

In my bare feet, admittedly somewhat unsteady at first, I made my way to a window that overlooked the backyard. I wiped away the frost on the pane with the heel of my hand. The fog had lifted. The temperature had dropped, and to my utter astonishment, everything was dusted with at least one inch of pure white snow. I rubbed my eyeglasses clean with the hem of my nightgown. I looked again. There was no mistake about it. It had snowed. The skies were overcast in all the splendor of thick Confederate-gray flannel. Most importantly, it was still flurrying. Every place my eye fell to rest looked like a drawing from Currier & Ives.

What do you think I spotted? One bright cardinal posed on a snow-covered branch of an old live oak. His beautiful red plumage stood out against all the white. He seemed to perch there just for me to admire him. I tapped on the window to get his attention. He saw me, held his head to one side then the other, and flew away. A childish laugh of delight escaped my lips. We had a white Christmas! A red bird! It was simply spectacular.

My own fog started to lift as the previous night came back to me in living color. Christmas Eve had been an unmitigated disaster. I doubted my family would be able to pull off a merry anything . . . although Pearl had assured me over and again that she had a foolproof plan. She promised that everything was going to turn out all right. Talk was easy enough. I had yet to see any positive results. Oh! All the unnecessary pain they inflicted on one another! Why? I hoped and prayed with all my heart that Pearl was right.

To be honest, I had grave doubts. I realized it was time to align myself with Barbara. This family needed a matriarch immediately. I didn't want to interfere too much, as it would undermine Barbara's authority, ineffective as she had been till now. Pearl couldn't be the matriarch—she was already dead and leaving soon anyway. It truly was beyond Barbara's time to take the podium. I would help her. What could I do?

After some consideration, I decided it would be best to act as if nothing untoward had occurred on Christmas Eve. I would go down for breakfast, be pleasant to them all, and assess the situation. That assessment would tell me what, if any, further actions were necessary. If Pearl's plan failed, I would take my family aside with Barbara, one at a time. Together we would give them this old dame's version of a walk behind the barn.

"Best to get this show on the road," I said to no one other than the room itself.

I wondered what effect the snow would have on the course of the day. Now, in many places, one inch of snow is nothing, a mere trifling bother. However, in the Lowcountry, it's enough of a catastrophe to quarantine Charleston, South Carolina, from the rest of the world, as though we already weren't. I could only recall several snowfalls in my entire life. All of them were less than six inches. Nonetheless, *one* inch was enough to bring everything to a screeching halt.

Any severe weather meant the highway authorities would close all the bridges and overpasses, especially during the high winds of a hurricane or a tornado watch. But one inch of snow? Oh, my goodness! You would have thought there was plague out there in the streets spreading like kudzu! The governor would declare a state of emergency. Any and all roads with the slightest slope would close until workers could scrape it aside and spread sand. The truth was that Lowcountry snowfalls usually melted by early afternoon. Everyone had a jolly slushy holiday while the children built tiny snowmen from snowballs. As this was Christmas Day, almost every place of business was closed anyway.

I decided to talk about the weather when I got downstairs, as it was probably the only safe topic there was to broach.

I was dressed in a beautiful white wool dress and a matching jacket with gold-rimmed pearl buttons down the front. The buttons were symbolic, I thought. I decided on a pair of very low-heeled pumps with rubber bottoms so, should I decide to step outside, I wouldn't slip. They were of a dull metallic color, classic yet still very practical. I arranged my hair in my customary chignon and decided the day called for perfume. I had not worn perfume or cologne in months, if not years. So with a spray of something that smelled like jasmine, I began to descend the stairs to the kitchen, thinking I looked pretty sharp for a lady of my age.

It was almost eight o'clock. Surprisingly, the house was still, except for the smells from the kitchen, evidence that Pearl was already on the job.

As I carefully descended the stairs, I passed through the hall, straightening pictures as I arrived at one, then another. Everything was still cockeyed from the monster of last night's craziness. I took heart. It was a new day. By golly, I was going to do my level best to see that it was one filled with hope.

The dining room looked beautiful. The table was set with green-banded plates glazed with crackle finish over large hand-painted magnolias. The glasses were dark green crystal. Where had Pearl found them? They had been my wedding dishes. Pearl, the treasure hunter, had probably decided to use them to remind me of Fred and happier days. I ran my hand around the rim of one of the plates. I thought of how Fred had loved these dishes—so irrefutably Southern in their design. Fred loved history, all things Southern, and me. I missed him then so much that I was certain I could feel him next to my shoulder. When I turned to try to catch a glimpse of him, he was not there.

My eyes shifted back to the table. In the center was my mother's Victorian silver epergne, another piece of our family's formerly elegant life that I had not seen in decades. Its high center bowl was piled with spotless red apples, polished to a glossy sheen, and green grapes, which draped over the sides. The three side dishes overflowed with nuts of all kinds, all of them nestled in beds of Spanish moss. The table looked absolutely perfect. It hailed a return to stylishness and gentility, courtesy of Pearl's thoughtful creativity.

I swung open the kitchen door. There she stood. I had no intention of letting on that I thought she was leading us straight to a family apocalypse.

"Merry Christmas!" I said. "Did you see the snow?"

"Merry Christmas to you, too, Ms. Theodora! Merry Christmas! I saw it but I can't take credit for it!"

"Don't tell me you . . ."

"No'm, the white stuff was a gift from a saintly friend of mine in the weather department," she said, with a grin. "How about some tea?"

Pearl was baking a breakfast casserole made from layers of egg-soaked bread, cooked, crumbled pork sausage, topped with grated sharp Cheddar cheese. I had not enjoyed one in ages. I couldn't wait to taste it. No doubt it would be fantastic. A cookie sheet of biscuits was ready to go into the oven, a pot of grits was simmering on the stove, a bowl of fresh fruit salad was on the counter, and a pot of strong coffee was brewing. The air was so aromatic that I couldn't understand how anyone could sleep through it!

"Hot tea would be lovely. With cream. Thank you. You are too much, Pearl! Everything looks so . . . I don't know, like it used to in the old days! Thank you so much."

"I miss the old days, too, 'eah? It's a pleasure to re-create them."

"Yes." I paused and sighed, wondering if any of the beauty of it all was rubbing off on my family. "Is anyone up yet?"

"Not that I know of, but Santa came." She raised the gas under the teapot to bring it to a boil.

"How about that? Of course he did. Heavenly days, I am so ancient, I forgot to even look! I'll be right back!"

I turned around and hurried along to the living room. When I was a youngster, Gordie and I would race to see our loot at the crack of dawn! We would knock each other out of the way, grabbing our stockings from the fireplace, dumping their contents onto the floor . . . that was a thousand years ago. The memory of that excitement faded fast when I reached the living room.

There stood Barbara, frumpy and forlorn in her quilted bathrobe, adding a few things to the Christmas stockings that hung over the fireplace. My heart sank. There was no bicycle under the tree for Andrew. Had Camille forgotten or was it hidden somewhere else? If one didn't appear by supper time, I'd draw him a picture of one. We would go shopping together tomorrow. I would gladly be his extra Santa.

"Merry Christmas, sweetheart," I said to my daughter, and gave her a light kiss on her cheek. "How are you feeling this morning?"

"Well? Pretty glum, to be honest. Merry Christmas, Mother," she said. Her eyes were puffy and rimmed in red. She must have cried all through the night. "I am still struggling with what exactly happened at dinner. Honesty is one thing, but there was cruelty, just appalling cruelty, coming from my husband, the children, my brother . . . I just don't know what to do about it. I have never felt so inept! Even my little granddaughter was just awful to poor Andrew . . . what should I do?"

"We have to talk to them about forgiveness and about kindness. Oh, my darling girl! I can see that you have suffered so much and I blame myself for a lot of it."

"Why? You're a wonderful mother!"

"No, sweetheart. I've been a lazy thing. There were so many times I could have reached out to try and help you and I didn't. Ever since Fred . . ."

"I know. Things have never been the same."

"Yes, but my mourning is behind me now, Barbara. It really is and I want you to be assured that I will stand up for you whenever you want me to. Camille needs help. Lynette needs your support. We have to talk to them and help them lay down some new guidelines for their children's behavior, especially Teddie. And George? I'll be glad to give him . . . well, I'll give him *hell* if you want me to. I will, you know!"

With a wail that could wake the dead, like they ever slept anyway, Barbara hugged me and hugged me with all her might until I thought she might crack one of my ribs. As she sniffed loudly, I flailed around in the confines of this massive bear hug in search of a tissue, found one, and handed it to her. Finally, she stood back, blew her nose, and smiled.

"What about Cleland? Could you give him hell, too?"

"We are about halfway home, on this," I said.

"If you say so," she said. Obviously she had no earthly idea what I meant.

"You've got a secret weapon and you don't even know it."

"What?"

"Well, there's my will, you know. But it really isn't a *what* it's a *who*!"

Barbara lit the lights on the Christmas tree. It started blinking like it had gone mad. We both stood there, looked at the crazy thing, and then with the tip of my shoe, I pulled the plug right out of the wall.

"Awful, isn't it?" Barbara said.

"Worse than awful," I said. "Come with me. It's time to talk to Pearl."

Reluctantly, Barbara followed me to the kitchen, pulling her belt tight around her waist, shuffling in her slippers.

"I sure could use some coffee, I guess," she said.

It was strange that Barbara was not dressed for the day. It was unusual in our home to come downstairs in your pajamas unless you had the flu or some ailment. But she was understandably depressed and probably letting decorum go for one morning. But, like the young people say, Barbara needed to get her act together. *Tout de suite!*

We were about to make that happen.

We pushed open the door to the kitchen.

Pearl said, "Merry Christmas, Ms. Barbara! Why, don't you look nice!"

I looked back to see my daughter dressed in a gorgeous white knit skirt and cashmere sweater. Her hair was beautifully blown out, her makeup appeared to be professionally applied. She looked more stunningly beautiful than I could ever remember. Even on her wedding day!

I burst out in a laugh and said to Pearl, "You're going to kill us all from shock if you don't stop it, you know."

Pearl clapped her hands and slapped her thighs as she buckled over in a riotous fit.

"Merry Christmas, Ms. Barbara! I thought you needed something new and snazzy to wear!"

"Merry Christmas, Pearl . . . what?" Barbara looked down at her clothes and shoes. Her face was incredulous. She was completely stunned. "How could this . . . I mean, what in the world?"

"We need a little chat," Pearl said. "Time's a-wasting! You need reinforcements!"

As Pearl and I told Barbara the truth about everything, she listened carefully, asking us to repeat many things. She was positively as dumbfounded as I had been to learn Pearl's identity and her capabilities, and she was more than willing to cooperate with us to pull her family together.

"Did you say . . ."

"Yes, I did," Pearl would say. "Here's what you have to do . . ."

Right before nine, Cleland appeared at the door freshly shaven but wearing an old sweater and rumpled trousers—a most uncelebratory ensemble, given the occasion.

Barbara smiled, handed him a cup of coffee, exactly as he liked it prepared, and said, "Merry Christmas, sweetheart! Now go dress in a sport coat and tie. We're going to church. Gosh! You smell good! Get the others up, too. Tell them no Santa until after church, to dress nicely, and come for breakfast right away! Okay?" She smiled at him as sweetly as she could, stood up on her tiptoes, and gave him a kiss on the cheek. "Thank you, sweetheart!"

Cleland, not knowing what to say, wished her a Happy Christmas and kissed her cheek in return.

"You sure look, um, different!"

"Thanks! The kids?"

"Uh, sure thing," he said, and turned to leave. "Um, don't you think they're going to raise the devil? Church? Late Santa?"

"Let them! Blame me! This is *my* house!" Barbara said.

Cleland looked at her in surprise. The tiniest of all smiles crept across his face. "Good for you!" he said as he disappeared behind the door.

"R-e-s-p-e-c-t! One down and just a few more to go," Pearl said, licked her forefinger, and swiped the air with a single stroke on an imaginary scoreboard.

"I can't believe he didn't fight with me about it!" Barbara said.

"Hmmph," Pearl said. "He was a boy before he was a man, wasn't he?"

"Pearl's right," I said. "What she means is that every man still has a little residue of his boyhood heart that needs to be taken care of in the same way every woman still has a little girl in her."

"When she's got the time to find her!" Pearl said, laughing.

"Isn't *that* the truth?" Barbara said, and laughed as well.

Barbara yanked and pulled the belligerent pocket

doors to the living room closed so that the tree and all the gifts were hidden from view. Pearl spread breakfast on the sideboard. Soon my family members, dressed in appropriate clothes and thinly disguised hostility, appeared in the dining room, served themselves, took their places at the table, and once again, devoured the meal.

"I don't feel like going to church," George said, pugnacious as ever.

"George?" Lynette said quietly. "I think it's important for Teddie."

How could he argue with that?

"I think it's important for us to pray together as a family," Barbara said. "No matter what you believe. We have so many blessings . . . besides, we have a white Christmas. Just the short walk to and from church will be beautiful!"

How could *anyone* find fault with *that*? It appeared that we were finally making some headway, but there came the hiccup. The conversation reverted to where it had left off on Christmas Eve.

Lynette, having shamed George into attending church, decided to remind him of something for which he should beg forgiveness while there.

"I still cain't be-*lieve* what you said to me last night, George!"

"Get over it, Lynette," he said. "How about what you said to me?"

"My brother and his lovely wife . . ." Camille said, drawing up the side of her mouth in criticism, looking at me.

I gave her a stern face. My "enough is enough" speech was on the tip of my tongue, when Barbara stood.

"All right now. Let's stop all this evil this instant. I have something to say." She turned to Camille and nodded to Cleland, George, and Lynette. "Here's how it is. First of all, Camille? You are my only daughter. Sweetheart?" She said the word so nicely it was heartwarming. "Let's face facts. You've got problems."

"Like you're perfect?" Camille retorted with a definite edge of defiance in her voice.

"Hush. That's not for you to say. I'm the *mother* of this family. It's time we all shape up or there won't *be* a family. Unfortunately, George and Teddie are right about your money issues, but it was contemptible to say anything about it. The fact is that for years I've been giving Grayson money to pay your bills. He was so demoralized by your overspending and . . . well, to be frank, your drug abuse, he couldn't take it anymore. The only reason he didn't file for divorce and sue you for custody is that he loves you. He wants you to seek help. He loves you, Camille. So do I. And we love Andrew, but Grayson *adores him,* Camille. With all his heart. Right after New Year's, you are entering a treatment program. I'm taking care of Andrew. He'll go to school in Charleston. It's all ready arranged."

"See?" Teddie smirked.

"Close your insolent mouth, little girl," Barbara said in an even tone. "From this moment on, you will mind your manners and have some respect for your elders or there won't be any Santa for you! At all!"

As though she had been slapped, Teddie's angry eyes filled with tears. She pouted, crossed her arms, displaying every kind of snippy body language short of throwing herself on the floor and having a full-blown tantrum. Everyone ignored her except George, who stunned the family and her by saying, "Cool it, kid. Your grandmother's right." George may have been insufferable sometimes, but he was smart enough to smell a change in the political wind.

"Grayson cares?" Camille said. Finally grasping what Barbara meant by entering treatment, she sputtered, "Wait a minute. I'm not going any-where."

"Yes, you are. By the way, I've invited Grayson for dinner this afternoon. There are enough pills in your purse . . . well, to stock a *pharmacy*! Keep only enough for the next six days and give me the rest. And your credit cards. You will do this for the sake of your own family."

"I'm not so sure . . ."

"Yes, you *are*," Cleland said. "You will do as your mother says. For the sake of your family."

Apparently, Cleland had purchased a ticket for the bandwagon, too!

"Okay," Camille said, looking at Andrew. It was easy to see that she was filled with self-doubt over her ability to kick her addictions. However, when she weighed trying to do so against the possibil-ity of losing Andrew, there was only one choice to make. "I'll do it. I can do it."

For some inexplicable reason, I believed she would. I could see she wanted to reconcile with Grayson. I knew she loved him. Most importantly, she had taken the first step toward accepting that *she* was the problem, not everyone else.

Barbara turned her attention to George.

"Now you listen to me, son. Teddie is your

daughter and Lynette is your wife. End of story. You are a family, too. I am putting you all on notice. You will get along, respect each other, and on January fifth, I am sending you all to a family counselor. I'll come to Charlotte to go with you if I have to. Do you understand?"

"So will I. Listen to your mother, George," Cleland said. "She's right."

Cleland was exhibiting all the signs of an inspired epiphany. His support wasn't *everything* I wanted for Barbara—I'm talking about fidelity and love—but it was a darn good start. Barbara beamed with confidence.

"Lynette, I have the name of someone I want you to talk to about anything that's bothering you . . . bullying, dieting, parenting, respect . . . you just name it. She will help you sort it all out. Now would anyone care for another biscuit?"

"Yes, I believe I would," I said. Barbara and I smiled at each other with such warmth and compassion that I felt myself flush with pride.

I pressed the buzzer under my toe. Pearl appeared in her black dress, ruffled apron, and starched crown. She smiled and smiled.

"What can I get for y'all, Ms. Barbara?"

She had deliberately given her attention to my

daughter as an affirmation of her newfound authority.

"Everything is perfect, Pearl. I just wanted to thank you for a wonderful Christmas breakfast."

"You are entirely welcome, Ms. Barbara! Merry Christmas everyone!"

"Merry Christmas," they replied with mixed enthusiasm.

"We had better get our coats on!" Barbara said.

The bells of churches all over Charleston were beginning to peal.

Resigned to the new order of the day, Teddie, George, and Camille grumbled their way to the coat closet. Andrew, Lynette, Barbara, and Cleland were more eager.

"The sooner we get there, the sooner we'll get home and find out what Santa brought," Lynette said to Teddie.

"Santa. Big deal," Teddie said. "Who cares about that old bunch of bull?"

"Miss? We'll have no more of that kind of talk!" Barbara said, but sweetly.

Having received more reprimands in twenty-four hours than he had in thirty-something years, George mumbled a stupid joke. "Who died and made our mother the boss?"

"You really don't want to know the answer to that," I said. "Now run along like a good family. Say a prayer for me, all right?"

"You aren't coming, Mother?" Barbara said with a trace of worry in her voice.

"You don't need me this morning. Pearl does," I said.

She nodded to me, trusting my decision, and gave me a kiss on the cheek.

"I love you, Mother," she said. "So very much."

It had been a long time since I had heard those words. I could feel my heart give a little lurch in my chest. I wanted to cry from joy.

"I love you, too, Barbara. I am *so* very proud of you! Now scoot!"

Pearl was right behind me at the front door. We stood together watching them all sashay down the slippery sidewalk. We saw Barbara and Cleland come to a standstill. She put her hands on her hips. We couldn't hear what they said to each other. I would ask her later. He put his arms around her. It appeared that at least for the moment, he had agreed to behave himself.

When they were out of sight, Pearl turned to the manger scene. She shot an eye to me.

"One gust of real wind and that thing's gonna be a pile of toothpicks," she said.

It was true. The shelter was listing to the west. There was no baby in the manger. It was a pitiful display.

"What are we going to do about this?" I said.

"Hmmph! Watch this . . ." Pearl inhaled. The little building righted itself toward us. Lights appeared all along its edges, inside and out. Then, in the wink of an eye, there was a swaddled baby doll lying in the manger.

"That doll is the hottest ticket on the toy market. That Teddie is going to holler her head off when she sees it. I gots the whole wardrobe and everything for it under the tree."

"She says she's too old for toys," I said with delight.

"Hmmph!" Pearl, in imitation of the most uneducated street child of the day, made the most brilliant statement of her entire visit. She said with a burst of laughter, "She be messing with she own head, too, 'eah?"

"Right! You're so right! That poor child! But aren't they all? What's next?"

"That *tree*!"

"Whoo hoo! Let's go!"

We hurried inside and pulled open the living-room doors, which, given their age combined with their condition, usually resisted over a tugging. Today, though, it was like some unseen hand had greased the tracks they rolled on. Maybe one had! Nonetheless, we stood back, staring in horror at the abomination before us. It was hardly the White House.

"Holy hairy cats and mangy dirty dogs! That is the ugliest thing I ever did see in my whole life! Before, during, or after!" Pearl said. She started to laugh. "Oooh! Help me, Lawd! Come on, Lawd! We gwine fix dis now! OOOH! Let's go!"

She took a very deep breath, waved her hands in the air over her head, snapped both fingers. The tree disappeared in a burst of smoke. In its place stood a regulation balsam fir, well over ten feet in height, lit with hundreds of minuscule gold glowing lights, strands of pearls looped all around it. All of our family's distinguished ornaments were hung in just the right spots. It was a magnificent feat, and without question, it was the most beautiful Christmas tree to ever grace our home.

"Pearl! It's gorgeous! I've never seen . . ." I gasped. "Pearl! Where are all the rhinoceros ballerinas? Those ugly elves?"

"Gone! Poof!" She looked at me with the expression of an imp, which wasn't easy for her to pull off, given her size.

"Pearl?"

Oh, she was a she-devil when she wanted to be! I knew Camille would come undone to see her tree destroyed. We would have trouble all over again!

"Gotcha! Didn't I? Well, I was gonna send them to the big furnace in the sky, but I put it in the family room instead! All that crazy stuff is back there!"

Not wasting a moment, she snapped her fingers, and the fireplace cleaned itself in an updraft. A new pile of logs lit themselves. In an instant, the drafty old room crackled with warmth. The mantel over the fireplace was laden with old-fashioned garlands. Wreathes decorated every window. Each had a red satin bow. Everything was reminiscent of my youth.

"Ms. Theodora? That's the same ribbon. Recycle! Let's show them how to do this 'eah thing right!"

"I'm with you, baby! What's next?" I felt like I was thirty-five!

Pearl stared intensely at all the wrapped packages under the tree. New ones appeared and they began to shift shapes and relabel themselves. That was quite a sight to behold!

All the wrapping paper became an opalescent ivory color and the boxes were now tied with red satin ribbon. I began to see a theme emerging. This was Pearl's Christmas.

As I followed her through the hall to the dining room, she pointed a finger at the stair rail and at the large hall mirror. They were immediately swagged in greens and ribboned in red satin. She paused for a moment to look in the hall mirror while she adjusted the greens.

"I'll be done 'eah soon enough! I gots to get dinner on the table, iffin that's all right with you? Hmmph!"

"Who are you talking to?" I said.

"The meter maid, that's who. Time's running out! Now let's get going. They gwine be home in less than an hour!"

"What can I do to help?"

"Nothing! You *know* you don't have to do a thing—no, wait! Where's your grandmama's Bible?"

"Heavens! I think it's in the bottom drawer of the sideboard! Why?"

"What kind of a question is that? What in the world is it doing in there?"

"What do you think? Because my heathen family

can't deal with looking at it! Probably makes them feel guilty, bless their hearts."

"That's your job, then. Fix it like your mama used to do. I'll go make the Reconciliation Eggnog."

"The *what kind* of eggnog?"

"Reconciliation! I gots to be sure when they *make up* that it *sticks*, don't I? Hurry now!"

Before she left me she eyeballed the hall table. Our family's crèche set materialized from nowhere. It was surrounded by greens and votive candles.

"Hmmph!" I said.

"Hmmph, yourself!" she said, laughing.

When Pearl disappeared behind the kitchen door, I got down on my knees to dig around in the bottom buffet drawers. I finally found the Bible in the heaviest drawer, the most difficult to open. There were piles of wrinkled place mats, stubs of old candles saved in case a hurricane blew out our electricity, paper cocktail napkins and napkin rings that we never used. When at last I found it and lifted it out from all the rubble, I figured as long as I was already on my knees I might as well offer a little prayer, so I did. Silently I said, *Lord? If You see my Fred, can You please tell him I said Merry Christmas, that I love him? If it's not too much trouble, can You ask him to make himself useful today, You know, to do what he can to help us? That goes for all my other dead friends and relatives, too. Thank You, Lord, Amen.*

My knees gave me a fit as I struggled to get up from the floor. Happily, I made a fortuitous rise without mishap.

I ran my hand across the red leather cover of the Bible. A flood of memories came back to me— looking at the pictures with Gordie long before we learned to read, how our grandmother read passages to us, how the story of Adam and Eve had scared us half to death, the beautiful calligraphy, how I marveled at the formation of the letters and the gold leaf when I learned to write in cursive. That same Bible had been as much a part of our day-to-day activities as my mother's cast-iron skillet.

I looked at the corner table where it used to rest for the Christmas season. I decided that was where it should go this Christmas day as well. The table was covered with silver frames filled with pictures of family vacations and other landmark events. They could all go in a drawer for the remainder of the season. I wondered if anyone would object. If they did, I would say that this day was not about remembering playing around on a beach, catching a fish, or seeing the Eiffel Tower. Christmas was a serious occasion. The Bible belonged on display. Period. I needed a silver tray on which it would rest, so I went toward the kitchen and the door swung open.

"'Eah!" Pearl said, handing me the exact one I wanted.

"Thanks," I said, thinking it was lucky for me the tray didn't come flying right through the air. It could have cut my head right off!

I put the tray on the table right in the center, opening the Bible to the Gospel of Luke, where my favorite story of the birth of Jesus was found. I looked around for extra candleholders. Finding none whose removal wouldn't make a table or a nook appear to have been robbed, I went to Pearl.

"I need—"

"I know." She pointed to the counter, where four silver candlesticks and four bayberry tapers waited.

She lifted the large bowl of eggnog and placed it on a tray. With less energy than it takes to extinguish a candle, she blew the kitchen door open to pass through. I shook my head at her otherworldly antics for the thousandth time since her arrival, took the candles and candlesticks, and followed her to the dining room.

"I've got ham biscuits and pimento cheese sandwiches to hold them until dinner is ready," she said. "Remember! They need to drink a cup of this!"

"Think it will do the trick?"

"Ms. Theodora? My God and my Gullah heritage ain't failed me yet, so I imagine they is still up to the task!"

"Lord, I hope so!" That was a prayer for divine intervention, not a blasphemous remark. "So, tell me, Pearl. What's for dinner?"

"Oh! My old sweet friend! What's your favorite Christmas dinner you ever had?"

"Me?".

The walls started to rattle, there were feet stomping overhead, and all the pictures went crooked again!

"I guess I ain't the only one asking!" she said, waving her arm at the walls as the pictures righted themselves and the house became quiet again.

"Or the only one who's hungry! Goodness! Let me think! The most delicious dinner I can recall right now was when I was about eight. My grandmother got it in her head that we were going to have a traditional English Christmas-day dinner. It wasn't easy in those days to find a good piece of roast beef or a fattened goose; at least that's what I remember them saying. Of course, there was no goose to be found, so they settled on roast beef."

"Hmmph! You think I don't remember? *Who* do you think cooked that meal?"

"Oh! Of *course*! *You* did!"

"That's *right*! Minted peas with little tiny white onions, mashed potatoes, Yorkshire pudding . . ."

We started to laugh again. Oh, by golly, this time we laughed until tears were streaming down our faces, whooping until some impatient, unseen force seemed to give Pearl a nudge.

"Oh, fine! Fine!" she said to the ceiling.

I looked at her, knowing that message meant we only had a short time left together. The thought of it made me want to break down and cry enough tears to fill the Ashley River. The Cooper, too.

I looked at my wristwatch. "Five minutes, maybe ten. Then they'll all be here!"

"What are you worried about? Let's close these living-room doors."

We slid them together with the sound of a pleasant thump. Pearl went to the kitchen once again to see about what magical event of hers was next to come. I lit the candles around the Bible and all the candles in the dining room. I wondered what Barbara, Cleland, and all the others would say when they returned to see the house all redecorated.

I toddled down the center hall, back to the family room. Lo and behold! Moving Camille's tree—which was now a lime-green fake tinsel model—back there had been a stroke of genius. It shimmered, caught light, throwing it back all over the room. In that milieu, a big-screen television, high-def you know, headphones, a desktop computer, oversize leather couches, recliners, stacks of DVDs, CDs—all that twenty-first-century tangle of wires and noise that usurped family time—well, in that milieu, Camille's tree was just the perfect thing. In fact, it gave an atmosphere of wacky good humor to the whole room. Perhaps I would suggest they leave it up all year!

Before you could say Robert E. Lee, I could smell roast beef. My stomach started to growl. It had been years since I was as hungry as I had been since Pearl came back. In the next minute, I heard the front door open. They were home. Pearl and I hurried to meet them—she from the kitchen, me from the family room—and we all nearly collided by the front door.

"Hi! Is Santa ready now?" Teddie said, with renewed interest.

"Almost! Come! Let's hang up our coats," Barbara said.

"Give me everything," Pearl said. "Let's make a quick stop in the dining room!"·

No one resisted, not that I expected them to object to any of Pearl's instructions. They were still *somewhat* bewitched from last night.

I ladled the eggnog into cups. Barbara put a ham biscuit and a small pimento cheese sandwich on each plate.

"Cheers!" I said to Cleland and to Barbara. We touched the sides of our cups. "Merry Christmas!"

They all drank and drank and drank until the bowl was half emptied. No one seemed anxious to open their gifts. The eggnog was obviously working.

"What's going to happen to them?" I whispered to Pearl as Barbara listened.

"They gwine say they are sorry and *mean* it. Then they gwine gain two pounds!"

Pearl laughed so wide we could see that she didn't have a single filling in her teeth. I had not ever noticed that before. In fact, I distinctly remember that when I knew her as a child, she had a few missing teeth in the back of her mouth.

"Who's your new dentist?" I said.

"My dentist? That woman is a saint!" she said, laughing again. Barbara looked at me. Still halfway unbelieving of the truth, she laughed, too.

"How was church?" I asked.

"The choir was fabulous! I prayed with great fervor for the quick and the dead," she said, winking at Pearl. "But I think I sprained my ankle when I skidded on the snow."

"I caught her so she didn't fall," Cleland said. "Thank goodness!"

That was rather noble, I thought. It also meant that they'd gone to church and come home arm in arm! Another good omen!

Pearl said, "I'll be right back." In the time it took to walk through the kitchen door and back out again, she reappeared with a walking cane. Naturally, it was white accented, with a mother-of-pearl handle. "This might help the reconciliation."

Barbara looked at it and laughed. Raising it over her head, she turned to the others. "Y'all better watch out now!"

How do you like that? It seemed that along

with confidence, Barbara had developed a sense of humor! I could not have been more delighted!

"I'd like to make a toast!" Cleland said.

Everyone stopped, looking in his direction.

"First, I'd like to thank Pearl for this delicious eggnog. In fact, thank you, Pearl, for *all* the delicious food we have enjoyed since your arrival. Things have been, well . . . incredible."

Cleland's summation was the understatement of the century.

"Here, here!"

"Most especially, I'd like to thank my lovely wife, Barbara, for many things, not the least of which is tolerating my . . . well, bad choices and poor attitude. I realized today that I have been wrong about many things. I just wanted to say in front of everyone that I am sorry. Barbara? I ask your forgiveness. Given a second chance, I would like to try to be the model husband you deserve. I don't want to be on the receiving end of any corporal punishment! Seriously, I would like to be a better father and grandfather, too! I would."

Honey? You might as well have announced that King Henry VIII was at the front door with a box of chocolates and a Christmas pudding! Stunned, everyone followed suit. George shook his father's hand, saying something to the effect of *let's start over.* Cleland gave George a warm, backslapping hug. I thought they would both start blubbering. Teddie and Andrew put their arms around Cleland's waist and squeezed before the waterworks could commence. When they hugged George he was so moved that he wiped his eyes with the back of his hand.

Just as Barbara put her arms around Cleland and kissed him right on the lips in front of the entire world, the doorbell rang. Camille answered it. In swept Grayson, who, by the way, was born into this world the color of milk chocolate himself, riding on a frosted white bicycle (yes, it looked like a pearlized finish) that was dripping with red and green ribbons and balloons, tooting the horn that was attached to the handlebars. Andrew ran to him, literally squealing with excitement.

"Daddy! Daddy! Wow! It's exactly what I wanted!"

"Oh, Grayson!" Camille threw her arms around Grayson's neck, looked into his eyes, and said, "Merry Christmas, sweetheart! I love you! Things are going to change. I promise! Things are going to change. I am so sorry. So sorry about everything."

He ran his hand down Camille's hair, held her chin, and said, "I love you, too, baby! Don't worry. We're smart enough to figure this all out. Doesn't love always find a way?" Grayson turned the bicycle over to Andrew and ruffled his curls. "You probably shouldn't ride this in the house. Merry Christmas!"

"Thank you! Thank you!"

Andrew was out the door and down the street in a heartbeat. No coat, no hat. Who cared?

"I saw it at the bicycle shop in Lenox Square, sitting right up there in the window. I thought it looked like something our boy might like!"

"Wouldn't you know it? I've got another one—a brand-new blue one in the garage!" Camille said. "It is exactly the same!"

"For me?" Teddie said. "Please? Please?"

Grayson and Camille, who, at this point, had their arms around each other's waist, looked at each other and said, "Sure! Why not? Have at it, sweetheart! Merry Christmas!"

Teddie blew past us. Within minutes, she was zooming down the sidewalk, chasing after Andrew. Her parents' generosity and their permission to be a child allowed her to become one again.

"Thanks!" George said. "That was very nice of you!"

Lynette said, "And we thought she didn't want toys anymore! Shows you what we know!"

George and Lynette were standing by the doors to the living room, also embracing, all smiles. Things were finally shaping up. I was so tired from the stress of it all that I felt like I was a thousand years old.

I went to the kitchen to see what Pearl was thinking.

"Didn't I tell you that they would be all right? Hmmph! O ye of little faith!"

I sat down at the counter and looked at her. She knew what I was going to ask before the words came out of my mouth.

"Pearl? Take me with you when you go. I'm so tired of living. I'm all done here. I want to be with Fred."

She looked up to the ceiling and then back at me.

"Can't do it. It ain't your time."

"Heavenly days, Pearl. Of what possible use can I be to anyone anymore? I ache from head to toe. I'm so weary. I can't hear, I forget so many things. I know I'm a nuisance . . ."

Pearl sat down next to me, took my hand in hers. She closed her eyes as though she was in prayer. I closed mine, too, searching my heart, trying to feel

Fred's presence. I felt warm all over, the same way I had felt as a young girl when I met him for the first time. I was so lonely for him.

"Ms. Theodora? You gots to understand this. When we go ain't up to us. I can do *this* much . . ." She stopped speaking, closing her eyes.

I nodded. "What? What?"

"I can try my best to be there when your time comes and I can put out the word that you're on the way."

"That's it?"

"That's it."

"That's not much."

"*'Scuse me?* How 'bout the last few days?"

"Extraordinary! Absolutely extraordinary!"

"All right, then, let's get our priorities straight, 'eah? Let's go open some presents!"

We gathered everyone toward the living room, except for Camille, who went outside to call for Andrew and Teddie.

Blocking the living-room doors, Barbara said, "We will wait for the children."

Barbara was absolutely right. I heard them approaching, laughing and high-spirited, delighted with their bicycles. They tumbled through the door, cheeks red from excitement and the cold.

Teddie held the baby doll tightly under her arm.

"Gigi! Look what I found in the manger!" she said. "It's like a miracle! You can't get this doll *any-where*!"

It's not like *a miracle,* I wanted to say, *it* is *one.*

"Maybe Santa put it there!"

Teddie looked at me, wide-eyed, with no guile at all. She said, "Do you *really* think so?"

"You *know* I do!" I was thrilled to see the light in her eyes.

"Why don't we see what else there is?" Barbara said, sliding back the doors. "You've all been so patient . . ."

When their eyes swept the room, there was a collective gasp. Then dead silence. I didn't know *what* they thought. The time between seeing it and remarking on it felt like an eternity.

"It's magnificent," Barbara said. "Isn't it?"

"It's beyond words . . ." Lynette said.

"What happened to my . . ." Camille said.

"Family room," Barbara said. "Like the White House? We can have more than one tree, sweet-heart, can't we?" Using her cane with all the poise of a queen, she knelt by the gifts and started hand-ing them up to Cleland. "Want to help me, dear?"

"Absolutely! Here, George! This is for you! Ca-mille? This is for you . . ."

All the packages were distributed, opened, and everyone shivered with surprise. Beyond the requisite bathrobes, slippers, sweaters, and books, there were mysterious gifts for every member of the family. Barbara received a beautiful pearl-and-diamond ring from Cleland that he had no memory of purchasing. Barbara gave Cleland pearl-and-diamond tuxedo studs and cuff links that she claimed never to have seen. In addition to doll clothes and accessories, Teddie received a page of stick-on earrings that, when applied, made her ears appear to be pierced. Lynette and George, who were sitting on the sofa holding hands, saw the disappointment in her face.

"Come here, sugar," Lynette said to her. "Daddy just said if you want to pierce your ears next summer, it's okay with him."

"Really?"

"Yep, I just want you to be old enough to take care of them, that's all. If you want your ears pierced . . . ah, what the heck? Come here."

Teddie crawled up on to Lynette's lap. George produced a satin pouch from his pocket, handing it to Teddie.

"I couldn't tell you where these came from. They were in my jacket pocket after church. They were just *there* . . . strangest thing . . ."

Teddie dumped the contents of the pouch into her palm, shrieking with excitement.

"Pearls! Oh, Daddy!"

She hugged his neck so tight I thought he might choke. But he did not.

He said, "A young woman has to have a little bit of jewelry, right? Promise me not to grow up too fast . . ."

Teddie kissed her father on the cheek and then Lynette too.

"Promise! Keep these for me, okay, Mama? I gotta go play with Jackie!"

Jackie was the name of the new and highly coveted doll. It appeared that for the moment Teddie was more than satisfied to be treated as a little girl.

The gifts of pearls continued. Lynette received a strand of white baroque pearls. Camille opened a double strand of smaller cultured ones. George and Grayson opened wristwatches with mother-of-pearl faces and leather straps. I found mother-of-pearl eyeglasses for me and a beautiful coffee-table book about pearls. I was the only one who was not surprised besides Barbara, who had come to accept that anything was possible. In fact, we were *all* coming to accept that anything was possible.

In addition to the simple laptop for Andrew

and a basic photo printer and digital camera for Teddie, a last minute ingenious gift from Barbara to encourage collaboration, there was a signed first edition of John Steinbeck's *The Pearl* for Andrew that came with special instructions on a card.

It read: *Andrew, This is a priceless possession. You will have to give it to your parents for safe-keeping. Read it together with your whole family. There's a lesson in here for everyone. Merry Christmas! Santa.*

"Dinner is on the table," Pearl said from the doorway of the living room.

"Then let's go!" Barbara said, leaning on the cane to rise from her chair.

I put my arm around her for extra support. "What in the world did you say to Cleland?" I whispered to her. "He's a changed man!"

"I told him if he wanted me to wipe his drool when he was an old man, he had better be nice to me *now*!"

"That's all?" Cleland had been whipped into shape with the threat of poor geriatric care? I didn't believe it! Did *I* drool? Heaven forbid!

"Honestly? I forgave him for everything. I told him that I loved him with my whole heart, that I always had and always would."

"Mercy! What happened?"

"You won't believe this. He started to cry. He said he thought he had hurt me so badly that I would never love him again."

"And?"

"I told him the past was in the past, that I wanted to spend the rest of my life making him happy. I suggested he do the same for me. So we called a truce. You know what?"

"What?"

"He told me he thought I was beautiful. Do you know when the last time was that he used that word in reference to me?"

"Oh, my darling girl! When was the last time you were this confident and happy?"

"Touché!"

Barbara gave me a little squeeze around my shoulder. We went into the dining room together to have our Christmas dinner.

This time Cleland's offering of grace was heartfelt and everyone bowed their heads sincerely. There were so many miraculous things that had occurred, it was impossible not to become emotional.

Pearl sliced the meat and served the dishes. To my surprise, my precious Andrew got up and went over to the Bible. In our family, it was understood that once you were seated for a meal, you did not leave the table without permission. Everyone, or at least it seemed that everyone, stopped and took notice. Was Andrew going to read aloud? The day had gone so well! I didn't want him to be humiliated or for the mood of reunion to be eclipsed by his reading problems.

"Come back to the table, sweetheart," I said.

"In just a minute," he said. "*Listen!* This is *exactly* what they read in church today." My great-grandson, that sweet child who had suffered so much ridicule, proceeded to read in perfectly enunciated English the following verse. " '*And the angel said to them, do not be afraid, for behold, I bring you good news of great joy which shall be to all people; for today in the town of David a Savior has been born to you, who is Christ the Lord. And this shall be a sign to you; you will find an infant wrapped in swaddling clothes and lying in a manger. And suddenly there was with the angel a multitude of the heavenly host praising God and saying, Glory to God in the highest, and on earth, peace among men of good will.*' How cool is that? This book matches the one in church!"

We were astonished for many reasons, mostly because for the first time we were witnesses to Andrew reading without one stutter or error. Camille jumped up, broke into tears, grabbing him by the shoulders.

"That was simply beautiful, son! Simply beautiful!"

Grayson lifted him in the air and deposited him back in his seat. He kissed the top of Andrew's head. "Well done, Andrew. I am so proud of you I could just burst my buttons!"

Even Grayson choked up and a tear or two escaped.

Everyone held up their glass in recognition of Andrew's accomplishment, saying something complimentary. I caught Pearl's eye.

"That was a little something extra from me," she whispered as she put my plate in front of me. "That boy's gonna be fine from now on! He's my favorite."

"We *are* all going to be all right," Camille said.

"Honey?" Barbara said. "All anybody in this life wants beyond good health and enough money to live is love and respect. I don't know about you . . ."

"We've got plenty of everything to go around," George said, finishing her thought.

Cleland chimed in with, "Yes, we certainly do."

You might imagine that everyone ate their dinner, relishing every single bite, and you would be right. As soon as they could be excused, the children went back to their Christmas toys. I could see them from where I sat. They were getting along better than they ever had.

The adults lingered at the table, talking about how important this Christmas had been, how glad they were that they had all aired their differences and confessed to one another. Most importantly, how grateful they were to one another to have been given another chance. I looked up to see Pearl in her red coat with her suitcase in hand. She put her finger to her lips, asking me to be quiet. She slipped out to the hall. I saw her say something to the children, who got up and followed her. I watched the children's faces, their expressions as awestruck as my own, as Pearl walked straight into the hall mirror and disappeared. They ran to the mirror, touching it. My tears began to flow. I got up from my chair and went to them. They were quivering with doubt and fear.

"Gigi? Did you see that?"

"Yes, I did." I was glad that they had seen what I had known for a long time, but I was also burdened with incredible sadness to know my friend was gone.

"How?" Teddie said. "How did it happen? It's not possible! Is it?"

"Well now, let's think about it . . . isn't Christmas a charmed time, when anything is possible?"

"Why are you crying, Gigi?" Andrew said.

"Because Pearl was the best friend I ever had in my whole life. She was."

I knew there would be rounds of discussions. Barbara would accept Pearl's arrival and the report of her departure because she had seen what Pearl could do. Cleland would want to hear the story again and again, and instead of a cocktail, he might opt for decaffeinated coffee for the recitation. Camille would commit herself to a stint in a rehabilitation program, from fear if nothing else. She didn't want some ghost coming back to get her! George would be incredulous but then say something like *Anything's possible in this crazy family.* We would all laugh at that. Grayson would say he had seen things like that all his life, that most people just wouldn't know a miracle was happening to them if it bit them on the nose! And Lynette? Our country girl, Lynette, would sum it all up with something like *Anything that could bring us all back together again can't be a bad thing!* They were all correct.

I went to bed that night as tired as if I had climbed Mount Kilimanjaro. Holding Fred's picture in my hands, I kissed it and pressed it to my chest. I would see him soon enough. There was no reason to rush my demise, as things around here were finally worth living for.

I slept hard. Without warning, Pearl's face came into view.

"So, tell old Pearl. How was your Christmas?" she said.

"Fabulous, thanks to you, old friend! I miss you already!"

"I'm always just a thought away, Ms. Theodora. Just a thought away. Don't worry about that."

"Well? Did you get your wings?"

"Hmmph. Don't know yet. I think I shouldn't have used so much Gullah magic or drunk up all that brandy."

"What does that mean, Pearl?"

"It means you fools better *watch* yourselves or I might just come back!"

"I would love it if you did . . ."

Smiling and wagging her finger at me, she faded away. I drifted into a blissful state of rest, thinking how wonderful it was that everyone I loved was only a thought away. I could live with that. I could live *for* it, too.

$\mathscr{A}$UTHOR $\mathscr{N}$OTE •

The recipes included in the first edition of *The Christmas Pearl* originated with my immediate family. Most notably, I used those of my mother, Dorothea Benton MacDaniel, and my sister, Lynn Benton Bagnal, whose fruitcakes were never, ever used as footballs. When those cakes were in the oven, the whole house smelled like heaven on this earth and that is no exaggeration.

I mentioned in passing to my family and friends that *The Christmas Pearl* was being reprinted this year and wondered if anyone had a recipe or two they might like to contribute. Well, I have friends and relatives from everywhere who take great pride in the astoundingly beautiful and delicious meals they prepare and serve, as they should. They were generous to share.

These are the soups, salads, casseroles, and treats we serve when we all get together for the holidays that are remembered and recreated from generation to generation.

Merry Christmas!

P.S. Special thanks to the Edisto Women's Club for the use of their recipes.

P.P.S. Forgive me, but I have to say that I think my cousin Judy Blanchard Linder's potato salad could be vastly improved with the addition of one half cup of chopped green olives. At least that's what my mother always said to her father, Theodore S. Blanchard, Sr., who said olives were disgusting. My mother thought the chopped onions he added overpowered the subtle flavors she favored. This difference of culinary opinion began around 1945 and continues today. My momma was right. Sorry, but she was.

ONE OTHER THING . . .

The use of all the photographs was so generously granted to us from the South Carolina Historical Society, for which my publisher and I are very grateful. If you want to slip a little something in their Christmas stocking, please send your gift to them at 100 Meeting Street, Charleston, South Carolina 29401. Or call (843) 723-3225 to support them in other ways. Many thanks.

She-Crab Soup

- 1 quart half-and-half
- ¼ teaspoon ground nutmeg
- 2 pieces lemon zest
- ½ stick butter
- ¼ cup crushed oyster crackers
- salt and pepper to taste
- 2 dashes Tabasco sauce
- 1 pound white crabmeat
- 2 tablespoons sherry

Put half-and-half in top of a double boiler with nutmeg and lemon zest and bring to a simmer. Cook for a few minutes at simmer. Steam should rise from milk, but do not boil. Then add butter and continue to simmer for 15 minutes. Thicken with cracker crumbs; season with salt and pepper and Tabasco sauce. Add crabmeat.

Allow to stand on back of stove for a few minutes to bring out the flavor. Just before serving, add sherry. This same soup can be made with shrimp, which should be ground.

SERVES 6

5-Alarm Chili

By Gina Asaro-Collura

- 1 pound ground turkey
- 1 pound ground bison meat
- 1 10-ounce can black beans (drain liquid)
- 1 10-ounce can pinto beans
- 1 can diced tomatoes with chili pepper
  (found in the Mexican food aisle)
- ½ sweet onion, chopped
- chili powder
- cumin
- hot salt (Morton's brand)
- Frank's Hot Sauce
- 2-3 red and green chili peppers
- 2 tablespoons olive oil
- sour cream (if desired)

In Dutch oven, pour 2 tablespoons olive oil. Add chili peppers (whole) and chopped onion. Heat. Add cumin, chili powder, and hot salt. Sprinkle Frank's Hot Sauce on top.

Add ground turkey and bison, mixing meat together. Cook thoroughly for about 20 minutes (covered), so hot mixture soaks into meat.

Stir every few minutes. Liquid will form (good sign). Uncover and add diced tomatoes. Stir.

Add both cans of beans (drained). Stir. Cook on low for 20 to 30 minutes.

Serve with a dollop of sour cream on top.

SERVES 4 TO 6

Jamie's Chicken Tortilla Soup

By Jamie Siekierski-Benton

- 4 to 6 cooked chicken breasts
- 2 cans chicken broth
- 1 medium onion diced
- 4 large tomatoes (or two cans of tomatoes)
- ½ jalapeño pepper (remove seeds if you don't like spicy foods)
- ½ cup chopped fresh cilantro
- ½ teaspoon minced garlic
- ½ teaspoon fresh pepper
- 1 teaspoon salt
- ½ teaspoon chili powder
- 1 teaspoon celery salt
- ¼ cup Masa flour mixed with 1 cup of cold water
- 1 cup corn (if desired)

Boil chicken breasts or use a pre-cooked chicken (from your local grocer) and chop into small pieces. In a large pot, combine your chopped chicken, broth, jalapeño, cilantro, garlic, and onion and bring to a boil for 15 minutes. Turn your heat to low and add remaining ingredients except flour. Let simmer for at least 30 minutes. Add your Masa flour to 1 cup of cold water in a container that has a lid and shake until creamy consistency. Slowly pour into pot while stirring. Soup will become slightly thicker.

Serve in a bowl topped with tortilla strips, shredded jack or cheddar cheese, and sliced avocado.

Chilled Peach Soup with Raspberry Cream

By Glenda Pate

- 2 quarts peeled and chopped fresh peaches
- 1 teaspoon chopped fresh mint
- ½ teaspoon ground cinnamon
- ⅛ teaspoon ground nutmeg
- 1 cup dry white wine
- 1 cup peach schnapps
- ½ cup sugar
- 2 cups half and half

Stir together first 7 ingredients. Cook medium heat 15 minutes or until peaches are tender and liquid is reduced. Cool. Process in blender until smooth. Cover and chill. Stir in half and half. Top each serving with a dollop of raspberry cream.

RASPBERRY CREAM

- ¼ cup fresh or frozen raspberries
- ½ cup heavy whipping cream
- ½ cup sour cream

Process raspberries in blender until smooth.

Pour puree through wire mesh strainer, pressing with the back of the spoon. Discard seeds.

Beat whipping cream until stiff. Fold in puree and sour cream; stir well.

YIELDS 1 CUP

Garnish with mint leaf or raspberry puree.

SERVES 4 TO 6

Southern Vegetable Soup

(Also known as "cleaning out refrigerator" time)

By Glenda Pate

Southern vegetable soup uses no measurements — just basic ingredients and additional ingredients. Start with a very large stockpot — become creative!

- *tomatoes — fresh, frozen, canned (whatever); if soup becomes too thick, add more tomatoes!*
- *ham hock (include any bits of ham, even large "chunks" that may be left or near the bone)*
- *creamed corn (whole kernel may also be used)*
- *green beans*
- *butter beans*
- *carrots*
- *okra**

Start with tomatoes and ham hock in a large stockpot. If you don't have a lot of tomatoes, add a little water. Bring it to a boil and add all other ingredients except okra. Do not drain any canned vegetables. Add any or all of the additional list of vegetables (or any you have on hand) and salt to taste. Let the soup simmer until all the ingredients are done. Allow the soup to simmer for several hours (if you use dried beans, it will take much longer). About an hour before serving, add those ingredients marked with an asterisk (*).

Additional ingredients: English peas, black-eyed peas, lima beans, garbanzo beans (chick peas), onions, potatoes*, cabbage*, northern beans, navy beans, field peas, crowder peas . . .

*Add these ingredients last so they remain whole (not cooked to pieces).

Beet Salad with Mandarin Oranges and Goat Cheese

By Pat Martin

- 1 can sliced beets in water, drained
- arugula or spring mix salad greens
- 1 can mandarin oranges, drained
- ½ cup walnuts
- 4 tablespoons goat cheese, crumbled

Mix together everything except cheese. Dress with a raspberry walnut vinaigrette. Sprinkle cheese on top and serve.

Frances Mae's Hot Chicken Salad for Twenty

By Lynn Benton Bagnal

- *10 cups cooked chicken breasts, cut into small pieces*
- *10 cups chopped celery*
- *1 #2 can ripe olives, sliced*
- *1 bunch scallions, sliced, including stems*
- *5 cups sharp cheese, grated*
- *8 ounces sour cream (may use low-fat type)*
- *8 ounces mayonnaise (don't use low-fat type if you used low-fat sour cream)*
- *salt and pepper to taste*
- *lemon juice to taste (I usually use about ½ cup lemon juice)*

Combine first 4 ingredients in large bowl, with about half the cheese. Stir the sour cream and mayonnaise together, add lemon juice, then seasonings. Add mixture to other ingredients. Put into 2 greased 2-quart Pyrex dishes. Top with remaining cheese and some breadcrumbs.

Bake uncovered at 350°F until bubbly (approximately 30 minutes).

This recipe may be made the day before, storing in refrigerator.

Potato Salad

(Used to be Uncle Teddy's, now it's Judy's)

By Judy Blanchard Linder

- 5 pounds Idaho potatoes, boiled and cooled
- 4 hard-boiled eggs, diced
- ½ cup chopped celery
- ¼ small yellow onion, finely minced
- 2 heaping tablespoons sweet relish

DRESSING

- 1 quart mayonnaise (I like Hellmann's)
- ⅓ cup yellow mustard
- ¼ cup bacon grease
- 2 teaspoons salt
- ½ teaspoon pepper
- 1 teaspoon paprika

Peel and cube potatoes, then add diced eggs, celery, onion, and relish. In separate bowl, mix dressing. Fold dressing into potato mixture. Make sure the potato salad is well mixed. It will look as if there is too much dressing but the potatoes will eventually soak up the dressing. Chill overnight. Stir before serving.

Garnish before serving with sliced hard-boiled eggs and paprika, if desired.

SERVES 20-25
(RECIPE CAN BE HALVED OR QUARTERED)

Red Rice

- 6 strips bacon, cubed
- 4 tablespoons bacon grease
- large onion, chopped fine
- 1 small can tomato paste
- 1½ to 2 cans water
- 2½ teaspoons salt
- 2 to 3 teaspoons sugar
- good dash each of black and red pepper
- 1¼ cups of raw, long-grain rice

Fry bacon and remove from pan, reserving grease; sauté onions in 1 tablespoon of the bacon grease. Add tomato paste, water, salt, sugar, and peppers. Cook uncovered for about 10 minutes until mixture measures 2 cups. Cool to room temperature.

Add mixture to rice in top section of rice steamer or a Dutch oven. Cover. Add 3 tablespoons bacon grease; steam for 30 minutes, then add crumbled bacon, and loosen rice with a fork. Add more liquid if necessary. Cook 30 to 45 minutes longer.

SERVES 6 TO 8

Charleston Red Rice

By Brenda Brodie

- 2½ cups tomato juice
- 1 cup rice
- 1 medium onion, chopped fine
- ½ teaspoon salt
- ¼ teaspoon pepper
- 6 to 8 pieces bacon, fried and crumbled
  (may substitute ham or smoked sausage)

In double boiler or rice steamer combine all ingredients. Cook over medium heat until water in lower pot begins to boil rapidly. Reduce heat to simmer and cook until liquid is absorbed in rice pot.

Sausage Rice

By Brenda Brodie

- *1 packet Lipton dry chicken noodle soup*
- *2½ cups water*
- *¾ cup white rice*
- *1 medium onion, chopped fine*
- *1 package Jimmy Dean sausage*
- *2 chicken bouillon cubes*
- *salt and pepper to taste*

Add onion, soup mix, and rice to cooking dish prepared with cooking spray. Dissolve bouillon in cup of water. Add broth to casserole. In a skillet, cut sausage into small pieces while browning. Keep separating into smaller pieces. Drain sausage of grease. Add sausage crumble to casserole and remaining water. All ingredients should be covered with water. Bake in 375°F oven for about an hour or until all liquid is dissolved, then cook an additional 15 minutes.

Collard Greens

- 2 bunches collard greens (leaves will wilt as cooked)
- ¼ streak of lean or fatback of pork slices
- 2 14½-ounce cans chicken broth
- 3 cups cold water
- 1 teaspoon sugar
- ½ dried hot red pepper
- 1 teaspoon apple cider vinegar
- salt and pepper to taste

Wash greens two or three times to remove sand. Cut heavy bottom stems from leaves then chop or tear the remainder. As greens are being washed and readied for cooking, cook the pork slices in frying pan or in microwave for 3 to 4 minutes. Lift from grease when brown and drain on paper towel. Prior to cooking, place the pork and greens in a pot, cover with broth and water. Add sugar, hot red pepper, vinegar, and salt and pepper to taste. Cook in 6-quart pot for approximately 1 hour or in 6-quart pressure cooker for 25 minutes.

Greens can be cooked one to two days ahead of serving time and reheated.

TOPPING

- *1 cup chopped mild onion*
- *1 green bell pepper, chopped*
- *1 cup apple cider vinegar*
- *4 rounds chopped jalapeño pepper*

Mix all ingredients together. Do not heat this mixture, as it should be crisp when served. This may be made a day ahead and kept in the refrigerator if covered tightly. Yum!

SERVES 6 TO 8

Favorite Sweet Potatoes

By Fredda Thompson

- 3 to 4 large sweet potatoes
- ½ cup sugar
- 2 eggs, beaten
- ½ teaspoon salt
- ½ stick butter or margarine, melted
- ½ cup milk
- 1½ teaspoons vanilla

Boil potatoes until soft and rub peelings off. Mash potatoes and combine with other ingredients in baking dish.

TOPPING

- ½ cup brown sugar
- ⅓ cup flour

- *1 cup pecans, chopped*
- *⅓ stick butter or margarine, melted*

Mix together all ingredients and spread on top of potatoes.

Bake at 350°F for 35 minutes.

Cheese Straws

- ¼ pound butter, room temperature
- 1 pound sharp cheese, grated
- ½ teaspoon salt
- ¼ teaspoon cayenne pepper
- 1¾ cups plain flour
- more cayenne pepper for garnish

Preheat oven to 350°F.

Cream butter and cheese with salt and pepper. Add sifted flour. Put in cookie press or chill, and then roll thin. Cut with 1- to 1½-inch round cutter. Place on ungreased baking sheets.

Bake for 15 to 20 minutes or until light brown. Sprinkle with cayenne to taste. Remove from baking sheets before they are cold. May be stored in tightly covered container.

YIELDS ABOUT 100

Biscuits

- *2 cups White Lily Self-Rising Flour* *
- *dash of salt*
- *⅔ cup vegetable shortening or cold butter*
- *⅔ to ¾ cup milk or buttermilk*
- *1 egg white mixed with 1 tablespoon cold water*

Preheat oven to 450°F.

Measure flour into a large bowl. Add salt. Divide shortening or butter into pieces and scatter on top of flour. Work pieces into flour with a pastry cutter, two knives, or your fingertips until pieces are about the size of BBs.

Make a hole in the center of the dough and pour in milk or buttermilk. Dough may be sticky. This is okay!

Turn dough onto a lightly floured surface. Knead gently for two or three strokes. Add a little flour if necessary to handle dough. Using a light touch, pat or roll dough to ½-inch thickness. Chill.

Cut with floured 2-inch biscuit cutter, leaving as little dough between cuts as possible. Gather remaining dough and reroll one time. Discard scraps remaining after second cutting.

Place biscuits on baking sheet with sides touching for soft biscuits, or close together but not touching for crispier sides. Brush with egg-white mixture.

Bake for 8 to 10 minutes, or until tops of biscuits are golden brown.

Serve hot out of the oven.

YIELDS 12 BISCUITS

*White Lily Self-Rising Flour available at www.whitelily.com

Chuck's Cast Iron Skillet Corn Bread

By Isabelle Mims

(Her husband is Chuck)

- *2 tablespoons Mazola oil*
- *1 cup flour*
- *1 tablespoon baking powder*
- *2 tablespoons sugar*
- *1 teaspoon salt*
- *1 cup yellow cornmeal*
- *1 egg*
- *1 cup milk*
- *2 tablespoons butter, melted*

Preheat oven to 450° F.

In a mixing bowl combine the dry ingredients.

In a separate bowl mix the egg, milk, and Mazola oil. Pour this mixture into the bowl with the dry ingredients. Stir it up.

Put 2 tablespoons butter in a cast iron skillet and place the skillet in the hot oven. When the butter sizzles, add the corn bread mixture.

Bake at 450°F for 25 minutes until the edge is crispy and the top is golden brown.

Place a plate over the top of the skillet and flip the corn bread onto the plate.

Serve with more *real* butter!

SERVES 10

Corn Fritters

Fred Scott's Recipe

(Glenda Pate's Uncle)

- *2 eggs*
- *1 cup milk*
- *2 cups flour*
- *2 cups drained corn*
- *2 tablespoons shortening*
- *3 teaspoons baking powder*
- *1 teaspoon salt*
- *1 teaspoon sugar*
- *¼ teaspoon paprika*

Beat eggs and stir in milk, flour, and other ingredients.

Drop from spoon into deep fat and fry until brown.

SERVES 6 TO 8

Hot Crab Dip

By Linda Manus

- 3 ounces cream cheese, softened
- ½ cup mayonnaise
- 8 to 9 ounces drained crab meat
- ¼ cup minced onion
- 1 tablespoon lemon juice
- ⅛ teaspoon hot pepper sauce

Beat cream cheese with mayonnaise until smooth. Stir in remaining ingredients. Spoon into small ovenproof dish.

Bake at 350°F for 30 minutes or until bubbly.

MAKES 1 CUP

Vidalia Dip

By Annette Jerwers

- *1¼ cups chopped Vidalia onion
  (or other sweet onion)*
- *½ cup mayonnaise (not Miracle Whip)*
- *1 cup shredded mozzarella cheese*
- *8 ounces cream cheese*

Mix all ingredients.

Bake at 350°F for 25 to 30 minutes, until bubbly.

Serve with crackers or veggies.

Chrourk Trausak

(Cambodian Cucumber Relish)

By G-Nell Winslow

- *1 English cucumber or 1½ regular cucumbers*
- *½ cup peeled, julienned ginger (about 2 ounces)*
- *2 shallots, thinly sliced*
- *⅛ red bell pepper, thinly sliced*
- *2 tablespoons white vinegar*
- *1½ tablespoons sugar*
- *1 tablespoon fish sauce*
- *½ teaspoon salt*
- *thinly sliced Birds Eye chilies, seeded (optional)*

Remove the ends of the cucumber. Without peeling it, pierce the skin with a fork all over so it will absorb the pickling flavors. Slice the cucumber as thinly as possible so that the slices are transparent. You should have about

2½ cups. Place everything in a bowl and mix thoroughly. Chill before serving.

For Southern tastes: Use 1 shallot for a double recipe. Cut the ginger into very small, halved julienned pieces. The Birds Eye chilies are extremely hot, so you may substitute a small amount of a fresh red chili pepper, very thinly sliced and reduce the fish sauce to ½ teaspoon.

Grammy's Chili Sauce

By Jamie Siekierski-Benton

- *1 dozen medium ripe tomatoes, peeled and chopped*
- *2 medium onions, chopped*
- *2 medium peppers, chopped*
- *1 bunch of celery, chopped*
- *1 teaspoon cinnamon*
- *1 teaspoon ground cloves*
- *1 tablespoon salt*
- *1 cup sugar*
- *2 cups vinegar*

Cook all ingredients together for several hours until thickened. Chili sauce can be used in meat loaf (1 cup to 1 pound of meat, stir in and mix). It can also be used over chicken or meatballs. Best if canned like any other relish and can be stored in refrigerator for a couple of weeks, since it contains vinegar.

Brenda's Tomato Chutney

By Brenda Brodie

- *1 pound brown sugar*
- *1 cup water*
- *1 cup cider vinegar*
- *2 large onions, peeled and sliced lengthwise*
- *2 red, green, and yellow peppers, sliced thin*
- *12 to 14 tomatoes, diced (or 3 large cans diced tomatoes)*
- *1 clove garlic, pressed*
- *2 tablespoons cloves*
- *2 tablespoons allspice*
- *2 tablespoons cinnamon*

Cook over medium heat for 30 minutes; then reduce to simmer for 1 to 2½ hours.

Good with pork, beef, or chicken.

Mexican Relish

By Cyndy McCormick

- 2 small cans chopped green chilies, drained
- 2 small cans chopped black olives, drained
- 6 green onions, chopped
- 4 large tomatoes, chopped
- 4 tablespoons olive oil
- 3 tablespoons red wine vinegar
- 1 to 2 tablespoons garlic salt

Combine ingredients.

Let set in refrigerator a few hours before serving.

Serve with tortilla chips.

Mother's Turkey Dressing

By Estelle Moody Hough Secrest

(Submitted by Isabelle Mims)

- 1 large loaf sliced bread
- 1 recipe corn bread (see recipe on page 182)
- 1 cup celery and leaves, diced
- 1 large onion, diced
- ½ stick butter
- broth from cooked turkey
- turkey giblets cooked in pan with water
- 2 tablespoons parsley
- 3 eggs
- 1 cup milk
- 1 teaspoon baking powder
- 3 hard-boiled eggs

Make corn bread in a cast-iron skillet in the oven. Let cool and crumble.

Sauté celery and onions in ½ stick of butter. Put broth from cooked turkey in with cooked giblets and water.

Slowly toast the bread in a warm oven to make the bread crispy. Let cool. Crumble the bread and the corn bread into a large bowl and mix together. Pour sautéed celery and onion into the bread and corn bread mixture. Mix together and add 2 tablespoons of parsley. Pour 3 cups new broth with giblets into the bread mixture.

Beat together 3 eggs and 1 cup milk. Add 1 teaspoon baking powder. Blend this mixture into the bread mixture.

Add salt and pepper to 3 diced, hard-boiled eggs. Add to bread mixture. Grease large baking dish with butter. Place turkey dressing mixture from above.

Bake at 350°F for about 45 minutes.

Thanksgiving Stuffing for 15-Pound Turkey

By Grammie Louise Pietromonaco

- 3 packages of breakfast pork sausage
- 3 pounds ground chicken or beef
- ¼ pound butter
- 3 cups chopped carrots
- 3 cups chopped celery
- 1 chopped large onion
- 3 cups chicken or vegetable broth
- 2 bags stuffing bread

Brown pork sausage and ground meat together.
Set aside.

Sauté all vegetables in butter. Place in large bowl. Add stuffing bread and broth.

Stuff into turkey and cook. Put excess stuffing mixture into separate pan and cook in oven. While turkey is cooking, add some turkey drippings to moisten the stuffing in the separate pan.

Cook at 350°F for 40 minutes.

Fruited and Glazed Ham

- 8 to 10 pound ham, bone in
- whole cloves
- ¼ cup Dijon mustard
- ¼ cup brown sugar
- 2 tablespoons plain flour
- small jar peach preserves
- large-size can pineapple slices, with juice
- small jar maraschino cherries, with juice

Preheat oven to 350°F.

Slice bottom of ham so it will lie flat in pan. Gently remove brown skin from ham. Score the fat and lean of the ham with a knife and garnish with cloves. Mix mustard, sugar, flour, preserves, ⅛ cup of juice from the pineapple slices, and ⅛ cup of juice from the cherries in a saucepan over low heat until thickened some-what. Spoon the sauce over ham.

Decorate ham with pineapples, placing a cherry in the center of each pineapple ring, holding in place with a toothpick. Bake for one hour, basting occasionally with any remaining sauce. Remove toothpicks before slicing.

Edisto Shrimp Boil

By Lynn Benton Bagnal

- 1 bay leaf
- 1 teaspoon salt
- 1 teaspoon black pepper
- 1 large onion, chopped
- ½ garlic clove
- 3 pounds Polish sausage cut in 2-inch pieces
- ½ cup butter
- 12 ears corn, fresh or frozen, shucked and halved
- 24 to 30 new potatoes, with skins on
- 4 pounds unpeeled, raw shrimp
- 1 sliced lemon
- 1 package Crab Boil (Old Bay or similar)

Fill 5-quart stockpot a little more than halfway with water. Add bay leaf, salt, pepper, onion, garlic, and sausage. Bring water to boil and cook 10 minutes. Add butter, corn, and potatoes.

Cook 10 to 15 minutes or until potatoes are tender.

Add shrimp, lemon, and Crab Boil. Bring to a boil and cook two minutes or until shrimp are tender and pink.

Drain water and serve on a platter or in a large bowl with cocktail sauce and plenty of napkins.

SERVES 10 TO 12

Chicken and Olives

By Jennifer Collura

- 3 tablespoons olive oil
- 3 cloves garlic
- 4 pounds chicken breasts and wings
- salt and pepper
- ½ cup sherry or white wine
- 2 tablespoons vinegar
- 20 sliced black olives
- 20 sliced Spanish olives

In frying pan, heat garlic and oil. Let brown.

Cut bone on the chicken breast into 2 pieces and throw away the tip.

Add chicken, salt, and pepper into pan.

Cook chicken thoroughly on both sides until golden brown. Remove from pan.

Into pan drippings, add wine (sherry), vinegar, and olives; add some water to make juicier.

Place chicken, juices, and olives into a baking dish.

Bake at 350°F for 30 minutes.

Breakfast Casserole

- 12 slices white bread, crusts removed
- 2 to 3 tablespoons butter, softened
- ½ cup butter
- ½ pound fresh mushrooms, trimmed and sliced
- 2 cups thinly sliced yellow onions
- salt and pepper
- 1½ pounds mild Italian sausage meat
  (out of casing)
- ¾ to 1 pound grated cheddar cheese
- 5 eggs
- 2½ cups milk
- 3 teaspoons Dijon mustard
- 1 teaspoon dry mustard
- 1 teaspoon ground nutmeg
- 2 tablespoons fresh parsley, finely chopped

Preheat oven to 350°F.

In a 9 x 13-inch baking pan, butter the bread with the softened butter and put aside.

In a skillet, melt the ½ cup butter and sauté the mushrooms and onions over medium heat until tender (6 to 8 minutes). Season with salt and pepper. Cook the sausage meat in same skillet breaking up the meat in small pieces as cooking. In a greased shallow casserole, layer 6 slices of bread, mushroom mixture, sausage meat, and cheese. Repeat layers ending with the cheese.

In mixing bowl, mix eggs, milk, mustards, nutmeg, 1 teaspoon salt, and ⅛ teaspoon pepper. Pour over the casserole. Cover and refrigerate overnight.

Before baking, sprinkle parsley over the top of the casserole. Bake uncovered for 1 hour or until sides bubble.

Serve immediately with a fruit salad and bread.

SERVES 6 TO 8

Shrimp Creole

- 2 medium-size onions
- 1 green pepper
- 1½ cups celery
- 4 tablespoons bacon drippings
- 1 large can plum tomatoes
- ½ teaspoon sugar
- 4 tablespoons tomato paste
- salt and pepper to taste
- 3 cups cooked shrimp

Coarsely chop onions, green pepper, and celery; sauté in bacon drippings until translucent. Coarsely chop can of tomatoes. Add tomatoes, sugar, and paste to sautéed mixture. Let mixture simmer slowly to thick consistency for 30 to 45 minutes. Add salt and pepper. Five minutes before serving, add cooked shrimp.

This should be served over cooked long-grain white rice. Creole seasoning salt may be substituted for salt and pepper.

SERVES 6 TO 8

Tedesco Grilled Tilapia

By Karen Tedesco

* 5 large pieces tilapia
* 2 large fresh lemons
* 2 fresh garlic cloves
* olive oil
* fresh parsley, cleaned and chopped
* salt and pepper

Rinse tilapia under cold water and dry. Drizzle olive oil on cleaned tilapia. Season with salt, pepper, and fresh parsley.

Sprinkle with 1 pressed garlic clove. Grill on high heat for a few minutes on each side.

In a separate dish mix:

- *3 tablespoon olive oil*
- *3 tablespoon water*
- *1 whole squeezed lemon*
- *fresh parsley*
- *1 pressed garlic clove*

Spoon over cooked tilapia and sprinkle salt and pepper to taste.

SERVES 4

Macaroni and Cheese

By Judy Blanchard Linder

- 3 cups elbow macaroni
- 1 pound mild cheddar cheese, grated
- 2½ to 3 cups milk
- ½ cup butter or margarine
- ½ cup flour
- 1 teaspoon salt
- ½ teaspoon pepper

Cook macaroni according to package directions until al dente.

Melt butter in 3-quart saucepan. Add flour, salt, and pepper. Cook on medium heat until completely mixed. Take pan off stove and slowly wisk in 2½ cups milk. Put pan back on stove and cook until mixture thickens and is almost at a boil.

In buttered 2½- to 3-quart casserole dish, combine drained macaroni, sauce, and ½ pound cheddar cheese. Add more milk if mixture is too thick. Sprinkle rest of cheese on top. Bake uncovered at 350°F for 30 minutes or until cheese is melted, bubbly, and slightly browned.

SERVES 8-10

Priscilla Martignette's World Famous Lasagna

By Joanne Martignette Benton

DOUGH INGREDIENTS AND SUPPLIES

- *3 eggs*
- *3 cups flour*
- *warm water*
- *bowl*
- *broom handle (must be solid and weighted)*
- *towel*
- *pizza cutter*

Sift 3 cups flour into bowl. Add 3 eggs, which have been cracked in separate bowl, to the flour and mix with hands (not with mixer).

While mixing with hands, add approximately ⅓ cup warm water, then knead dough. As dough begins to stick together, empty onto table and continue to knead, adding more warm water if necessary (don't make it too soft). Continue kneading dough until glossy, then hide under bowl for 15 to 20 minutes.

After dough comes out of hiding, cut in half and roll each half into a small circle with your solid broom handle, wrapping dough around handle and flipping in a back-and-forth motion until dough is light and lifts up when you blow under it. Let dough dry for 20 to 30 minutes on table. Once dry, cut with pizza cutter into thin straight strips.

Cook noodles for approximately 5 to 7 minutes in boiling water. Once cooked, take noodles out, lay them on towel, and pat dry.

FILLING INGREDIENTS AND SUPPLIES

- *large container Sorrento ricotta cheese*
- *2 to 3 eggs*
- *grated pecorino Romano cheese*
- *salt and pepper*
- *bowl*
- *grater*
- *spoon*

Empty ricotta cheese into bowl.

Crack two eggs in separate bowl and stir. Add to ricotta. If necessary, add third egg (but be sure it's not too thin).

In separate bowl, grate pecorino Romano cheese.

Add approximately ⅛ cup grated cheese to the ricotta cheese. Add ½ teaspoon salt and 4 shakes pepper.

Assembly Ingredients and Supplies

- *glass lasagna pan*
- *one package Sorrento solid mozzarella cheese*
- *sauce (see sauce recipe on page 215)*

Spread small amount of sauce on bottom of pan. Lay noodles, overlapping, across bottom of pan, then lay additional layer in opposite direction. Spoon ricotta mixture over noodles and spread evenly throughout pan. Add another layer of noodles (do not make it bulky).

Lay ¼-inch thick slices of mozzarella cheese on top of noodles. Spread sauce over cheese. Sprinkle additional grated Romano cheese over sauce. Add another layer of noodles. Add another layer of sauce, then sprinkle more Romano cheese.

*If you have followed Priscilla's instructions correctly, you should now be able to place lasagna pan on a cookie sheet with ½-inch water separating pans into a 350°F oven and cook for one hour, covered in aluminum.

Meatballs

- *1 pound hamburger*
- *4 eggs*
- *4 or 5 slices stale Italian bread, soaked in water,
  salt, and pepper to taste*
- *Italian parsley*
- *½ clove garlic, cut into small pieces*

Beat eggs. Add hamburger, bread (squeeze
extra water out of bread), salt, pepper, parsley,
and garlic. Mix well. Form into meatballs and
fry in hot oil until light brown.

PRISCILLA'S SAUCE

Sauté a small chopped onion in two tablespoons of oil until translucent.

Put a large can of San Mattero whole plum tomatoes through a sieve. Add to pan. Add one can of tomato paste, one teaspoon of pepper, and one teaspoon of salt. Simmer for one hour.

Sauté a pound of hamburger until brown. Place in sauce. Cook for 30 additional minutes. Add meatballs and cook until meatballs are warmed through.

Serve with lasagna.

Fondant

- 1 egg white
- 2 tablespoons cold water
- 2 squares unsweetened chocolate (melted)
- 1 teaspoon vanilla
- 3½ cups sifted confectioners' sugar (approx.)
- whole walnuts or pecans

Beat egg white slightly and add water, chocolate, vanilla, and enough sugar to make fondant take shape. Roll into small balls and put half a nut on each, pressing down slightly.

YIELDS ABOUT 3 TO 4 DOZEN

Light Fruitcake

- 1½ cups butter (room temperature)
- 1½ cups sugar
- 1 tablespoon vanilla extract
- 2 tablespoons lemon extract
- 7 eggs, separated and at room temperature
- 2 cups all-purpose flour
- 1½ pounds candied yellow, green, and red pineapple (approx. 3 cups)
- 1 pound red and green cherries (approx. 2 cups, cut in half)
- ½ pound candied citron (approx. ½ cup)
- ½ pound golden raisins (approx. 1½ cups)
- 3 cups coarsely chopped pecans
- 1 cup coarsely chopped walnuts
- ¼ cup brandy or apple jack
- additional brandy

You may add an additional cup of fruit, i.e., orange peel, dates, or coconut.

Preheat oven to 250°F.

Make a brown paper liner for a 10-inch tube pan or two loaf pans. Grease both sides and fit into pan(s). Cut and grease both sides of a top for pan(s).

Cream butter and sugar. Stir in extracts. Beat egg yolks and stir into mix. Fold 1½ cups sifted flour into mixture.

Combine fruits and nuts in a large bowl; dredge with the remaining flour (½ cup) and coat well. Fold this mixture into batter, gently. Beat egg whites until stiff; fold into batter.

Spoon batter into prepared pan(s). Cover. Place cake in oven over a pan of water.

Bake for 2½ to 3 hours or until the cake tests done. Remove from oven, take off cover, and pour ¼ cup of brandy over cake. When cakes are cool, remove from pan and carefully remove papers. Wrap cake in plastic wrap and store in airtight container for three weeks prior to serving. Store in refrigerator, opening once or twice to spoon 2 or 3 tablespoons of brandy over cake in order to keep moist.

YIELDS 24 SLICES

Sands

- 3 sticks butter, room temperature
- 18 tablespoons powdered sugar, sifted
- 4 tablespoons vanilla extract
- 2 tablespoons water
- 4½ cups self-rising flour, sifted
- 3 cups chopped pecans
- half box powdered sugar

Preheat oven to 325°F.

Cream butter and powdered sugar. Add vanilla and water. Gradually add flour. Stir in pecans. Form into rolls as large as your thumb. Bake for 15 minutes, or until lightly browned, on a greased cookie sheet.

Sift half a box of powdered sugar into a paper bag. While cookies are still warm, shake in the bag to coat. Let cool and store in a covered tin.

YIELDS 3 TO 4 DOZEN

Rum Balls

- 1 cup vanilla wafers (crushed*)
- 1 cup powdered sugar
- 2 cups chopped pecans
- 2 tablespoons cocoa
- 2 tablespoons light corn syrup
- ¼ cup light rum (or 3 tablespoons cream and 1 teaspoon rum extract)
- granulated sugar for rolling

Combine vanilla wafers, sugar, 1½ cups chopped pecans, and cocoa. Add corn syrup and rum. Mix well. Shape into 1-inch balls. Roll half in fine granulated sugar and the rest in the remaining chopped pecans. Do not bake.

YIELDS 3 DOZEN

*I "crush" vanilla wafers in the food processor or blender!

Nut Cake

- 3½ cups plain flour, not self-rising
- ½ pound salted butter, room temperature
- 3 cups sugar
- 6 large eggs
- 1 cup heavy whipping cream
- 3 cups chopped pecans
- 1 teaspoon vanilla extract
- 1 teaspoon lemon extract

Preheat oven to 325°F.

Generously grease a tube pan with Crisco and lightly flour.

Sift flour three times and set aside. Cream butter with sugar until light and fluffy. Add eggs, one at a time. Beat only until each disappears. Blend in 1 cup flour followed by ½ cup whipping cream. Repeat with 1 cup flour then ½ cup whipping cream. Add 1 cup flour. Coat pecans with remaining ½ cup flour. Carefully fold pecans into batter. Fold in vanilla and lemon extracts.

Add batter to pan, level it, and knock bottom of pan on the edge of the counter, once, to get out the air bubbles. Place in the center of the oven and bake for 1 hour and 15 minutes, or until it's medium brown on top and *begins to pull away from the sides of the pan*.* Remove from oven. Wait 10 minutes and invert on a cake plate. Do not cover until cool to touch.

*Important

Apricot Brandy Pound Cake

By Linda Stuckert

- 2 sticks (½ pound) butter
- 3 cups granulated sugar
- 6 eggs
- 3 cups all-purpose flour
- ½ teaspoon salt
- ¼ teaspoon baking soda
- 1 cup sour cream
- 1 teaspoon orange extract
- 1 teaspoon vanilla extract
- ½ teaspoon lemon extract
- ½ teaspoon rum extract
- ¼ teaspoon almond extract
- ½ cup apricot brandy
- confectioner's sugar

Preheat oven to 325°F. Grease and flour a 10-inch tube pan.

Cream the butter and sugar. Add the eggs, one at a time, beating well after each addition.

Whisk together the flour, salt and soda.

Combine the sour cream, flavorings, and brandy.

Alternately add the flour and sour cream to the butter mixture, beginning and ending with flour. Blend well.

Pour into the prepared pan. Bake for 80 to 90 minutes until the cake pulls slightly from the sides of the pan.

Cool in the pan for 30 minutes. Carefully invert on a rack, turn right-side up, and allow to cool completely before slicing.

Dust the cooled cake with confectioner's sugar.

Note: The cake is even better after 3 or 4 days.

SERVES 15-20

Ladyfinger and Spring Pudding Trifle

By Susan Collura

STRAWBERRY COULIS

- 2 cups strawberries, quartered
- ½ cup sugar
- 1 teaspoon lemon juice

MANGO COULIS

- 2 cups peeled and cubed mango
- ½ cup sugar
- 1 teaspoon lemon juice

SPRING PUDDING

- 6 cups cubed angel food cake, torn into 2-inch chunks (can substitute ladyfinger cookies)
- 2 cups sweetened whipped cream
- 2 cups each cubed mango and cut strawberries

Combine ingredients for each coulis.

For strawberry coulis, combine ingredients in a small pot, bring to a boil, and simmer. Puree until smooth.

For mango coulis, combine ingredients in food processor until smooth.

In trifle dish, layer 1½ cups angel food cake or ladyfinger cookies. Layer strawberries, then strawberry coulis, then cake/cookies, then mangoes, then mango coulis. Repeat until trifle dish is nearly full.

Leave enough room to make a layer on top with whipped cream.

Chill until ready to serve.

Finnish Pancake

By Brenda Brodie

- 4 eggs
- ¼ cup honey
- ¾ teaspoon salt
- 2½ cups milk (use any milk, even half and half or skim milk)
- 1 cup all purpose flour, unsifted
- ½ stick butter

Put an iron skillet in oven at 425°F for 10 minutes with butter.

In a bowl, beat together eggs, honey, salt, and milk. Add the flour. Mix until well blended and smooth.

When butter is melted, pour batter into pan. Lower oven temperature to 375°F and bake for 20 to 25 minutes or until golden brown.

Serve immediately with your choice of fresh fruit.

Lemon Ricotta Cookies

(But they're not made with any lemon)

By Linda Wroblewski

- *4 cups flour*
- *2 teaspoons baking powder*
- *1 teaspoon baking soda*
- *1 teaspoon salt*
- *½ cup (1 stick) sweet butter*
- *1½ cups sugar*
- *2 large eggs*
- *2 teaspoons vanilla extract*
- *15 ounces part-skim ricotta*

GLAZE

- *2 cups powdered sugar*
- *3 tablespoons orange juice*

Mix flour, baking powder, baking soda, and salt.

In a separate bowl, mix sugar and butter with a mixer or food processor for about 3 minutes.

Add eggs, vanilla extract, and ricotta until well blended. Slowly mix in dry mixture. As you mix in the dry ingredients it will become a little stiff; so you may have to use another attachment to your mixer instead of the regular beaters. At this point, I use an attachment that has curves.

Cover and refrigerate overnight.

Form 1-inch balls out of the dough and place on a cookie sheet (parchment paper works nicely).

Bake at 350°F for approximately 10 to 12 minutes.

After cookies have cooled, dip in glaze and let dry.

Gan's Recipe for Sour Dream Sugar Cookies

By Jennifer Benton

This sugar cookie recipe was my paternal grandmother's. We called her Gan and now my grandchildren call me Gan. As children my brother, sister, and I saw her almost every month (she lived about 30 minutes away). We were her only grandchildren (my dad was an only child). Every December we would spend a weekend with her making Christmas sugar cookies. We would help her measure, mix, roll, cut, and decorate the cookies. Even as a teenager and young adult, I would visit every December to continue the Christmas cookie tradition. She died when I was 21, and I continued to make sugar cookies at Christmas with my sons and now with my granddaughter, Aubrie. When my twin grandchildren, Jones (middle name Michael) and Reagan, were one year old, they spent Christmas with Gan and Grampy. They sat in their high chairs and watched Aubrie and me make Christmas sugar cookies. I have a very old cookie cutter that was my Gan's that I still use.

- 2 eggs
- 1 cup oleo or Crisco (I use half and half)
- 1½ cups sugar
- 1 teaspoon baking powder
- 1 teaspoon baking soda
- ½ cup thick sour cream
- 4 cups flour
- 1 teaspoon vanilla extract
- ½ teaspoon almond extract
- ¼ teaspoon orange extract

Preheat oven to 375°F.

Sift flour. Stir together flour, baking powder, and baking soda. Set aside.

Cream together oleo, sour cream, and sugar until smooth. Beat in eggs and extracts gradually. Blend in the dry ingredients.

Chill dough for an hour. Roll out dough and use a variety of cookie cutters. Be sure to put flour on your rolling pin and dip your cookie cutter in flour each time you cut.

To add a variety of taste to some of the cookies, sprinkle fresh nutmeg into the dough. Sprinkle the cookies with sugar or other decorations.

Lift the cookies with spatula as you place them onto the ungreased cookie sheets.

Bake for 8 to 10 minutes.

Let stand on cookie sheet 2 minutes before removing to cool on wire racks.

Butter Brickle Dip

By Wendi J. Griffith

(As shared with Linda Manus)

- 8 ounces softened cream cheese
- ½ cup light brown sugar
- ½ cup sugar
- 1 teaspoon vanilla
- 6 ounces Heath Chips (almond toffee flavor)
- 5 tart apples
- 7Up or pineapple juice for marinade

Combine first five ingredients with a spoon. Chill for two hours. Shortly before serving, pare and slice the apples and cover with juice or 7Up to prevent discoloration. Drain on paper towels.

Arrange on a platter and serve.

Zeppoles

By Madeline Ragone

- *1 cup lukewarm water*
- *1 teaspoon regular dry yeast*
- *1 tablespoon sugar*
- *2 cups all purpose flour*
- *1 teaspoon salt*

Sprinkle yeast and sugar into water in a cup until yeast dissolves.

In a large bowl combine all ingredients, adding yeast mixture. Stir.

Cover with plastic wrap and let rise in warm area for 1½ hours.

Pour vegetable oil in heavy pot. Heat. When oil is hot drop dough by tablespoons into pot. Cook about 2 minutes.

Remove and sprinkle with confectioner's sugar.

Congo Bars

By Maxine Campbell

- 1⅛ sticks butter
- 1 box light brown sugar
- 3 eggs
- 2¾ cups unsifted self-rising flour
- 1 teaspoon vanilla
- 1 cup chopped pecans
- 1 cup chocolate chips

Melt butter. Pour over brown sugar and mix well, then let cool.

Add eggs one at a time, beating well. Add flour gradually. Add vanilla, nuts, and chocolate chips.

Spread batter in two 7x11 greased pans.

Bake at 350°F for about 30 minutes.

Cool. Cut into squares.

Bama's Bing Cherry Congealed Salad

(This was always a dish at Thanksgiving and Christmas)

By Lee Skidmore Wenthe

- *1 package raspberry Jell-O*
- *1 cup chopped pecans*
- *1 can bing cherries*
- *1 can crushed pineapple*
- *blackberry wine*

Dissolve Jell-O in ½ cup boiling water. Remaining 1½ cups liquid come from juice of bing cherries and the blackberry wine (enough to make a total of two cups liquid).

Stir in juice and wine after Jell-O is thoroughly dissolved (you'll probably have to stir to aid in dissolving).

Remove pits from bing cherries and break them in half. Add nuts and pineapple. Stir into Jell-O mixture.

Place in refrigerator until it sets.

Bama's Charlotte

(A summer dessert for six people)

By Lee Skidmore Wenthe

- *1 cup orange juice*
- *1 package Knox gelatin*
- *½ pint whipping cream*
- *½ cup sugar*
- *⅓ cup cold water*

Mix Knox gelatin and cold water. Heat ½ cup of orange juice. Mix gelatin/water combination in the orange juice. Add ¼ cup sugar. Let cool.

Whip cream until stiff, adding remaining ¼ cup of sugar as you whip.

When gelatin gets "ropey," fold over cream; then fold in remaining ½ cup of orange juice. Let it get thick, then put it in refrigerator until it is firm. You may have to "fold" ingredients again if they start to separate while chilling.

Serve in champagne flutes. Put a cherry or strawberry on top to make it look pretty.

Mint Julep

- *several mint leaves*
- *sugar syrup (2 or 3 teaspoons)*
- *crushed ice*
- *2 ounces Maker's Mark or a good bourbon*
- *1 sprig mint*

Crush leaves and let stand in syrup. Put into a cold, silver julep cup or glass and add crushed ice. Pour in whiskey. Stir, not touching the glass, and add sprig of mint. Serve immediately.

YIELDS 1 GLASS

Sugar Syrup

- *1 cup water*
- *1 cup sugar*

Melt in saucepan. Syrup can be stored in a Mason jar in refrigerator.

Mike Benton's Eggnog

By Jennifer Benton

- 6 eggs separated
- ½ cup sugar
- 2 cups milk
- 1 teaspooon vanilla extract
- 1 cup bourbon
- 1 pint heavy cream
- nutmeg

Beat egg yolks until light. Add sugar and continue beating until thoroughly mixed and light lemon color. Stir in milk, vanilla, and bourbon. Chill several hours.

Beat egg whites until stiff but not dry. Whip cream. Fold egg whites and cream into egg yolk mixture. Sprinkle with nutmeg.

Serve in festive holiday mugs or glasses.

SERVES 6 TO 8 PEOPLE, DEPENDING ON SIZE OF MUG/GLASS USED